WHAT HAPPENED AFTER KING ARTHUR DIED? WHO INHERITED THE GREAT SWORD EXCALIBUR? Could the heir be a runaway prince, his home now sunk beneath the sea, his only companions an uppity servant and a certain ragamuffin he found caught in a rabbit trap? Why would Destiny place so mighty a weapon in the hands of a young man reduced to acting for a living? Destiny has her ways, it seems. Prince Lowen of Lyonnais may be but a player strolling the roads of chaotic Dark Ages England, but he has a good heart and a winning manner, and prophecy is on his side. Arriving in a small northern kingdom which has lost its army and must therefore defend itself using tricks straight out of fairy tales, Lowen captures the heart of the king's daughter, and marriage beckons. But so does death. Already in love with the princess is Morgan, the most redoubtable knight in Britain, who has slain many of her suitors and seemingly would not mind adding Lowen to the list. Deadly combat must surely ensue. Swords will be wielded, and each has a deadly edge. And so may magic . . .

Prince of Nowhere

Prince of Nowhere

by PARKE GODWIN

2011

FIRST EDITION

ISBN
978-1-848632-81-3
978-1-848632-82-0 (signed edition)

Cover art by James Hannah.
Book design by Pedro Marques.
Text set in Sabon.
Titles set in HamletOrNot (by Manfred Klein / CybaPee Creations).

Printed in England by the MPG Books Group
on Vancouver Cream Bookwove 80 gsm stock.

PS Publishing Ltd
Grosvenor House
1 New Road
Hornsea, HU18 1PG
England
E-mail: editor@pspublishing.co.uk
Visit our website at www.pspublishing.co.uk

Contents

The glamour of theatre!

—

(or) don't give up your day job

As British kingdoms went after Arthur's passing, the Northern March was nothing to write home about, and the little village of Tye, huddled outside King Moraunt's castle was even less. Since Arthur's death news had been mostly bad, occasionally dampened by worse for a change of pace. Today was little different because of a disturbing prophecy that leaked from the castle like water from an old pipe. The sword Excalibur: Some said the knight Bedivere threw it into a lake. Others held he did not but hid the royal symbol somewhere for safe keeping, and every two-penny kinglet in the Isles itched to get his hands on it—for the good of the country, of course. Most frightening, the prophecy said it was somehow here in the Northern March.

For bedraggled little Tye, this warm September day wasn't all bad. Crops were safely harvested with no disastrous loss, and they were in a mood to enjoy themselves, which in Tye meant only slightly less suspicious and sour. They flocked to the village square, drawn by the skirling of a penny-whistle and drum. Travelling players had come, and there they were, three of them in bright coloured hose and tunics: a girl with startling, luminous eyes who told fortunes for a penny, an acrobat with the face of a sly but benevolent imp—and the nimble young leader of the tiny troupe who leaped up onto a wagon, spreading his arms in invitation.

"My noble dames and masters! Give us a moment's attention, I pray."

Always wary of strangers, the crowd listened doubtfully to this boy who had a commanding presence unusual in common players and whose clear voice smacked of Cornwall. Not many players came this far north; those that did were viewed with a jaundiced eye since they'd been known to steal sheep and the occasional stage-struck daughter. This youth had charm to spare and a vibrant energy that made one forget his ordinary looks. There was something about him that smacked of higher places and suspect education.

"He's no respectable commoner," a blacksmith muttered resentfully. "Wouldn't trust him."

"My name is Lowen." The boy bowed gracefully. "Right here today for a penny. Presenting for the first time in the Northern March, the sensational Bronwen and Gwinnoc, seer and acrobat. Take it, Gwin."

"Make way, make way!" Gwin trumpeted with a flourish, clearing a space before the wagon while a little girl tugged at her mother's sleeve.

"What's a acrobat?"

"A tumbler," the mother said. "He jumps in the air and rolls around like what you do at home. Ent worth paying for."

The boy Gwin took a short run and somersaulted neatly, landing on his feet agile as a cat.

"My son who is in the king's guard can do as well," an old woman sniffed disdainfully.

"Hopefully not in the king's presence," Lowen caught her up. "Gwin, you've a challenge. Second best just has to try harder. Dames and masters, a taste of our quality before we go on to play before King Moraunt, by whom we were summoned fresh from London."

"Not hardly." No peach without its pit, no audience without its heckler. This one had been nipping at enough parsnip wine to feel godlike and ornery. "Most like run out on a rail."

"Well, it beats walking," Gwin laughed. "Good citizens, please stand back. This trick is unpredictable. Once I'm airborne I've been known to stay up for an hour."

"No way!" the heckler jeered.

"Good sir," Lowen inquired patiently, "can it be you doubt Gwinnoc whose miraculous feats of levitation have astonished crowned heads from London to fabled Lyonnais?"

"Garn, caught you out," the heckler crowed. "There ent no Lyonnais. Not there anymore."

Confirmation from the rear of the crowd: "Washed away it was. Everyone knows that."

Lowen took up his small drum and smiled coolly at the dubious watchers. "So I've heard. Are you ready, Gwin?"

"Ready!"

A rapid tattoo on the drum. Gwin spurted forward, left the ground light as a blown leaf, and turned head over heels twice before landing to a few impressed *ohs!* But critics, like fleas, are everywhere.

"My son in the king's guard—"

"Ah, *stuff* your son in the guard," the heckler roared. "You, tumbler. What've you got we ent seen before?"

As Lowen, the slight, winsome Bronnie poised by the wagon had an air about her of better times, like an angel with a tarnished halo. "Nothing for it," she shrugged to Gwin. "You'll just have to defy gravity."

"Masters, a moment please. This is a feat that requires preparation." Lowen hopped down and drew Bronnie close with urgent advice. "Don't try this one. It doesn't always work."

"Well, mostly." Bronnie brimmed with confidence. "Getting him up is easy."

"Last time you couldn't get him down."

"The wind was against me," Bronnie sniffed. "Have some faith in things bigger than you."

"Just you're so unreliable." Lowen surrendered the point and vaulted onto the wagon again. "Masters and ladies! To banish your doubts forever"—Lowen paused for dramatic effect—"Gwinnoc will now perform the impossible."

Again from the eternal heckler with a loud belch. "Garn!"

Lowen sighed. "Oh, ye of little faith. Ready, Gwin? Banish doubt. Banish—*gravity!*"

Gwin raised his arms, but instead of a running start, he shot up in a backflip. All attention was on him though a sharp eye might have seen Bronnie's lips move silently and her hands move in a subtle dance. Gwin's body turned over in the air—and suddenly, as if time suspended

7

itself, slowed in mid-air, moving like a graceful swimmer underwater through three utterly impossible somersaults before settling on his feet to beam in triumph at his audience. "Impossible enough?"

The applause was more generous now, but not by much. They had seen miracles, as those things went, but then they had also seen water-into-wine and appearing rabbits. Miracles were fine first time around but only mundane repetition after that. If Lazarus resurrected twice, they might merely ask if he passed their deceased uncle on the way home.

Lowen produced his tin pipe, and to the sprightly tune Bronnie and Gwin flashed into a fast clog dance, arms stiff at their sides, feet flashing in unison. Bronnie halted with the music's end but Gwin pranced on, counting aloud.

"Gwin, stop," Lowen ordered. "Cease. Desist."

"One-two-three-four-one-two. I can't stop."

"Why not?"

"So when we dance again, I'll know left foot from right."

"No fear." Lowen leaped down from the wagon. "I'll teach you."

"All right." Gwin challenged, hands on his narrow hips. "I can never remember. How can you teach me?"

"Simple subtraction, and these good folk are my witness. Tell me. How many feet do you have?"

Gwin's brow furrowed; he looked uncertain. "Can I count them?"

"No fair," Bronnie ruled. "Quick answer."

"Uh . . . two?"

"Splendid," Lowen encouraged. "Now, if I take away your right leg, what's left?"

Gwin pointed to the remaining limb. "That's left."

"That's right!" Bronnie yipped.

Gwin silently appealed to the onlookers like a man confused by alien logic. "No, it's *left.*"

"You're right, it's left," Lowen affirmed.

Now Gwin had a hounded aspect. "I'm sorry I started this."

"Well, you did, so let's finish it. Slowly now. Lift your right leg and give it to me."

The limb was raised with an air of achievement and placed in Lowen's grasp. "How'm I doing?"

8

Bronnie clapped. "Bravo!"

"Right," said Lowen, still holding the leg. "Now give me the other one."

Wavering on one leg, Gwin gave it a game try. "I'm at the mercy of physical law."

"As usual I have to do everything." Lowen dropped the right leg and grabbed the left, neatly flipping Gwin on the ground. "*That's* your left."

"Thanks so much. Glad we cleared that up." Gwin rose, wiping mud and less pleasant matter from his tunic to a few guffaws from the crowd. "Don't applaud, just throw money."

"And how much?" Lowen leaped onto the wagon again. "A mere penny, friends. A penny for miracles. Presenting—Bronwen, seer and magician beyond compare."

"Ha!" from the persistent heckler. "If that brat's a magician, I'm a duck."

"In truth," Bronnie verified sweetly, "one would never mistake you for a swan."

"Bronwen, masters. The most famous pupil of the renowned weird women of Scotland—and we all know how good *they* are—Bronwen, who sees things to come will reveal your own tomorrows. Who'll be brave enough to see his future, wise enough to know it for his own?"

Once more the heckler was inspired to put in his tuppence. "Ent no magician."

Lowen bent on him a look of injured integrity. "Would I lie to an honorable man?"

"Yah, y'would. If she's a magician, tell her to conjure me a pot roast out of air."

"Shut up, fool," his wife hissed. "You want them to think us poor folk?"

"We are. MAKE ME A POT ROAST!"

Bronnie's expression darkened slightly as she gazed on the fellow. "Is that what you really want?"

An observant bystander might read her mood as dangerous, and Lowen did. "Don't," he warned out of the side of his mouth. "If it doesn't work, you're a fake. If it does, we're in trouble. Remember London?"

"Not to worry. There's only fireworks for a start. Just to scare him a bit." Bronnie stretched her hand out toward the man, fingers dancing intricately. "Right then, good sir. You—are—a—pot roast. ZAP!"

Out of the clear blue sky came a clap of thunder. A truly impressive lightning bolt speared down to bless the annoying heckler, or rather where he had been. At the feet of his long-suffering wife rested a covered pot, savory steam rising from it like a benediction. She lifted the lid. "My husband—he's a pot roast!"

"It worked all the way." Bronnie regarded her guilty hand with awe. "Shouldn't have."

Lowen saw an audience about to become a mob when they recovered. "Quick, change him back."

"That's the tricky part. Sometimes takes hours."

"Here we go again." Gwin snatched up his knapsack. "Can we manage a graceful exit?"

Lowen swept up his drum in one hand, Bronnie in the other and tried to smile at a crowd now less frightened than murderous. "Masters, ladies, no charge for this performance. We're a little late, so bless you and good day,"

"*Get that girl! She's a sorceress!*"

But the two had darted away down the muddy street. Gwin gauged the lowering faces before him and voted, like Lowen, for a swift change of locale. "And that, dear friends, concludes the . . . concludes our . . . 'Bye. Lowen, Bronnie, wait for me. *Wait!*"

The art of kingship

—

(or) never run a bluff without a buried ace

EVEN AS LOWEN AND BRONNIE FLED THE MOB and a vengeful grass-widow to a pot roast, King Moraunt of the Northern March faced an ongoing dilemma of his own: How to maintain a small kingdom with no army and little more than mice in the treasury. In later ages, kings and even presidents would solve this by declaring holy or patriotic wars, but Moraunt was a clear-thinking man for whom the game of poker might have been invented.

He looked a king head to foot as he entered the throne room. Tall enough to be impressive, just the right dignified sheen of silver in his hair, the correct commanding glint to his eye. His prime minister Veluvius waited by the throne with a parchment. "Hail to Moraunt, royal hawk of the north!"

"Yes, yes. This is business, not ceremony, and there's none to hear you. Where are those soothsayers?"

"They wait on you, Sire."

"Let them. First, what news from that Irish king?"

Veluvius unrolled the short declaration and cleared his throat, a pompous man with delusions of empire for his country, which Moraunt knew to be absurd for a humble little kingdom with holes in its shoes. Still, he valued the prime minister for his better qualities. Lean, unsmiling Veluvius was suspicious as a mean watchdog kicked more often than fed. Not that Moraunt mistreated him; Veluvius came by it naturally.

"Thus it is," he read. "King Kevin of Ulster, knowing Moraunt to have a daughter of marriageable age—"

"And a throne he'd love to gobble up."

"—sends his son Prince Brian to ask the hand of Princess Gerlaine so that our two lands, though separated by the sea, may be one in everlasting alliance and peace."

"Or else," Moraunt finished grimly. This Kevin sounded like all the others. "You'd think one of them might show originality now and then. Does he know our law?"

"Yes, Sire. He follows, saying Prince Brian will challenge the king's champion, Sir Morgan, according to our custom."

"If only we had an army," Moraunt yearned. "Even a small one." The last war, as wars tended to, cost the flower of his country, even the weeds. "We're a land of old men, women and children."

"Old foxes," Veluvius corrected. "Others have armies; we have brains and Morgan. Ten princes have come, ten has he dispatched or discouraged. When enough kings have lost an unacceptable number of heirs, they *must* give up on us. And they don't know we have no army."

"Very subtle, Veluvius." Moraunt slumped on his throne, looking doubtful. "What if they send their own without asking?"

Veluvius spread pale hands with proven self-satisfaction. "Economics, Sire. As long as we have an unmarried princess, it is cheaper to send a prince singing love songs."

"Good day, Father. You sent for me?" Princess Gerlaine swept into the chamber, sixteen and lovely as advertised. The dignity and reserve of her upbringing showed in her erect carriage but not the large share of her father's wit and a sharp sense of fun brimming just below the surface. She was followed by a strapping young knight, Sir Morgan, whom Gerlaine knew all her life for a Gibraltar of trust but a bit stuffy and worlds too serious.

"There you are," Moraunt greeted them. "We thought you should both hear. The soothsayers have word for us."

Gerlaine remembered them. "Those nice old men from the woods." Morgan bowed to the king. Muscled shoulders rippled under his scarlet gown. "Good day, Your Majesty. Another challenge?"

"From Ireland, yes. A Prince Brian. Hope you had a pleasant morning."

"A frustrating time, my lord. I've spent it proposing to the Princess Gerlaine for the hundredth time."

"And I have spent it refusing." Gerlaine regarded her lifetime companion with affection, but couldn't suppress a small giggle. "Dear Morgan, you're the handsomest knight I know."

"I'm the only knight we've got left."

"You're wise, mature, tremendously strong and unbelievably brave."

"Then of course you will marry me."

"Dear Morgan, when you leave a little room for improvement, I just may."

"Morgan," the king assured him, "it is my dearest wish and purpose that you and the princess will marry someday, but right now it's—well, inconvenient." "Politically." Veluvius nodded. "Ulster has sent his son Brian to ask her hand."

Morgan's response smacked as much of boredom as resignation." Another one. Wouldn't they just."

Veluvius turned waspish, a manner quite suited to him. "And possibly another war if there's no one to propose to. He must be allowed to challenge you." The prime minister's words went silken. "Afterwards, as usual, we'll send him home with flowers. Your Majesty, the soothsayers wait on you."

At his sign, two old men sidled in to bow before Moraunt. As they were not often consulted, these overdid their dignity and presentation like most small-fry officials, draping themselves in Druidical robes out of fashion for years.

"My lord," the first intoned gravely, "we have seen."

"We have heard," the second chorused.

"We have understood what was seen."

"A black bird fell dying out of the sky."

"We opened the bird and read its heart." They paused, hovering and uncomfortable.

Veluvius prompted: "And?"

The soothsayers hesitated, clearly reluctant. "Morgan shall fall under the sword of Arthur."

Morgan snorted. "Impossible."

The king's reaction was stronger. "Poppycock." Like all shrewd kings, Moraunt was a politician. The thought occurred that these two might have been bought by his enemies, but he dismissed that. They were loyal, dedicated, not that swift of mind, and enjoyed a comfortable living without bribery. "Excalibur was lost. What are you saying?"

The last thing Moraunt needed was Veluvius murmuring in his ear. "The prophecy."

The first soothsayer raised apologetic hands. "Would that we could bring better news—as we have in better times—but this cannot be denied. A prince has come from Lyonnais."

"Now you *are* coming out of the blue," Morgan scoffed. "That two-penny rock on the Cornish coast? It doesn't exist anymore."

Most true, the overdressed Druids verified. Recently destroyed by a curse, doomed Lyonnais sank into the sea.

The king didn't buy that either. "Nonsense, the sea ran over it in a storm. You can still wade there at low tide—if anyone would want to. What else have you to brighten our day?"

Nothing good from the sound of it. The Prince of Lyonnais was probably within the Northern March as they spoke, bearing the sword of Arthur. "And . . . the princess will love him and Morgan will fall."

"That'll be the day," Morgan huffed. "There *is* no Lyonnais."

The soothsayers mumbled something apologetic: A modern translation might render it as the way the cookie crumbled. "It is prophecy, Sire. Fare you well."

Moraunt dismissed them with a wave. "We thank you and will send the usual gifts. Do come again when birds yield better tidings."

Relieved to be done, the soothsayers scuttled out, leaving concerned silence in their wake. "Well," Veluvius broke it, "they have brought clearer prophecies in their time. The sword of Arthur . . . "

If her father was worried, Gerlaine was intrigued. "I'm going to love him? Fascinating. Well, unique anyway. A prince from a drowned land."

"Dripping seaweed," Morgan jeered.

"But coming for me. The others I never got to know, thanks to you, but this one I must meet."

"Gerlaine, it is a serious matter," Moraunt said. "Arthur was the one king recognized by all, even Rome. In the wrong hands his sword would have them coming not alone but in hundreds."

"To find us without an army," Veluvius lamented. "A plague notice would be better news."

"Oh, of course it's all rot." Gerlaine didn't sound wholly convinced of that. "But I'm to love him?"

"Though perhaps not be loved in return," Veluvius observed from experience and a mind that would search the Ten Commandments for loopholes. "This is politics, not passion."

"True," Moraunt agreed. "You'll learn that someday, daughter. Love is a luxury for the poor. We can't afford it."

From beyond the castle gates came the raucous blast of a hunting horn. Gerlaine threw up her hands. "Aha! My phantom Lyonnais?"

"No, that is an Irish horn," Veluvius second guessed. "They always sound a bit flat."

Moments later, the courtier Evan ap Evan bustled into the chamber a trifle out of breath, bowing to Moraunt. "Prince Brian, Sire, with a party of six horse—"

"And deepest respects from his father." Moraunt finished the too-familiar greeting with him. "Don't ask how I knew he'd say that."

"He seeks immediate audience, my lord."

Moraunt blew out his cheeks. "Well, *he* wasted no time. His old spider of a dad can't wait to see what the pickings are. If it weren't such a bother it would be a positive bore."

Morgan spoke over folded arms, ready for the inevitable. "I'll have my sword sharpened."

"Business as usual," Gerlaine noted plaintively. "Here we go again."

"Evan," said the king, rising, "Let's meet him in the courtyard; it makes a good impression. Veluvius, measure him at your first opportunity. We may need another casket."

Veluvius inquired of Evan, "Is he of an unusual size?"

"Big as a house."

"No problem, my lord. We have the extra large in stock."

"Splendid. No delay for carpentry. And Gerlaine?"

"Yes, Father? What shall I be this time, eager, startled or blushing?"

"Just try to look properly serious when he asks your hand. Last time you giggled."

"Oh, it's a serious business. Lose a war, win it back with a wedding."

"Or a funeral," Morgan muttered, already warming to the prospect.

"Mark this down, Gerlaine." King Moraunt paused on his way out. "Anyone can steal, but to be loved for it takes art. Come, Evan."

"Not Lyonnais," Gerlaine regretted. "Not yet. Pity. I'm very curious about this one. The prophecy said I'd fall in love with him."

"Oh hardly," Veluvius advised. "There are two kinds of prophecies: the tinseled sort that one believes in and the kind a ruler must use as a tool. With this one, frankly, I'm still trying."

Bracketed between Morgan and the minister, Gerlaine twirled suddenly in a gay pirouette. "And I perhaps would like to believe in this one for myself."

"Not very wise," Morgan chided.

"Dear, gallant Morgan, I'm tired of being wise." More than that, at sixteen, Gerlaine could be bored by many things and captivated by many more. Being a princess had its dull side, so, let logic go begging, the pure *girl* of her caught fire at the image of a prince from nowhere riding out of the west to claim her. Call it idealistic, unrealistic, the vision ignited Gerlaine's imagination.

"Do you know, my lords," she mused, "I have an odd feeling about this prophecy. Not good, not bad, just . . . strange."

To give her credit, Moraunt's child was wise beyond her years but not immune to a prospect shimmering with mystery and romance. The prophecy beckoned and whispered to her. *Lyonnais . . . Lyonnais.* What if he proved less than a paragon of romance; she could always improve him. What Gerlaine simmered with now, an Austrian dictator much later would forge to a stirring but disastrous slogan: Tomorrow the World.

"Princess, you are gloryfying," Veluvius warned.

Morgan glumly agreed. "Storyfying."

"But think, my lords." From gazing out of the casement, Gerlaine turned to them, shining and determined. "I have ever been a dutiful daughter, or if I forgot there was always you to remind me, Veluvius.

Did the people need food in a bad year? There was I, smiling and passing out the goods. A banquet, a baron's birthday? There I was, dispensing charm and gifts. I've been a princess for sixteen hemmed-in *you wouldn't believe how predictably boring years*!"

The force of it made Veluvius blink. "So?"

Men would never understand. For the first time, this was all happening for *her*, not some political fishing lure. Gerlaine danced away from the casement into a capricious bow. "So until he appears and proves dull as the rest of them, let me be a girl for a while."

Veluvius would have pronounced that radical and subversive, but at that moment King Moraunt returned, followed by a lumbering mountain of a youth in a tartan riding cloak with a small, flustered Evan ap Evan protesting in his long-striding wake: "But—but look here. Just because Morgan is on the premises doesn't mean you're to fight him this minute."

"And why not?" Brian demanded in a brogue hard as old cider. "Let's be done with it and have the wedding tonight."

Florid and loud, young Brian was already a legend, as he would tell you himself and usually did. In a dozen more ages his beefy kind would turn football into mayhem while young, and later go tearful and misty on Saint Patrick's Day, wearing green and warbling of wild Irish roses and a Cathleen Mavourneen they wouldn't know if she straight-armed them with a shamrock. "And where's the late Sir Morgan?"

"There's no rush, dear chap," Moraunt reminded him politely, "It is the custom to meet at sundown."

"I'll be married by then." Brian planted himself before Morgan. "Would this be him?"

"That is he, Your Highness," said the king. "I have the honor to present Sir Morgan, the royal and undefeated champion."

Brian's ham fist lighted on his sword hilt. "Now or later?"

"Later please," Moraunt protested mildly. "They've just tidied up and I won't have you hacking away around the furniture. Sir Morgan, Prince Brian of Ulster."

Morgan granted him a slight, stiff bow. "My lord."

"And incidentally the reason for your visit. My daughter, the Princess Gerlaine."

Brian was instant charm. "Ah, what a rose she is. And myself about to be her husband."

Gerlaine curtsied. "The Irish know how to flatter."

"And how to win what's beyond price. A ray of sunlight you are in a month of storms. Myself being the finest husband you could wish, I ask the king for your hand."

Gerlaine rewarded his proposal with a thin smile that tried for warmth but didn't succeed. "I've always admired self-confidence." Even more she respected King Kevin's threat gift-wrapped in Brian's presence. With no clear successor to great Arthur, every sub-kingdom was up for the grabbing before a new emperor could be found. Her father's strategy was shrewd; actually it was desperate. The few soldiers Moraunt had were trotted out and very visibly marched this way and that from the moment Brian entered the courtyard. With much practice they became quite good at it, swelling their clattering ranks with wives, sons, uncles, aunts and stray farmers hastily thrust into mail and helmets. The trick had worked so far, and there was always her unbeatable Morgan. If muscle-bound Brian was a chip off his single-minded father, the odds looked better than good once more.

Morgan and Brian were eyeing each other dangerously. Veluvius cleared his throat. "My lord, are you prepared to challenge our champion?"

"Well now, isn't that what I've been saying since I put a boot inside your gates?"

"It's a formality, dear chap," Moraunt told him lightly. "Just say yes."

"Yes!"

Morgan waited expectantly. "Your gauntlet?"

"My what?"

"Your glove—but you don't have one. Borrow mine?"

"Glove me no gloves," Brian bristled. "If it's a challenge you're wanting—that fly buzzing there."

The heavy sword seemed to leap into his hand and slice the air in one fluid motion. The other hand, as neatly, caught first one installment of the former insect, then the other. Brian dropped them in Morgan's hand. "There's my challenge."

Morgan regarded the late fly. "Not bad for a country boy." Casually he tossed the two fragments into the air as his sword flashed out too quickly for the eye to follow and whirled twice. Morgan made four quick catches. He sheathed the sword and with deliberate care dropped the four quarters one by one at Brian's feet. "There's my answer. You're on."

Brian was impressed but laboured not to show it. "When you'd be trying something larger . . . "

"Any time, Irishman."

"My lords." Moraunt stepped between them. "I have said later. Veluvius?"

"You will meet at sunset," the prime minister announced. "The weapon will be broadswords."

"He's done already," Brian promised. "Was I not born with one in my hand?"

Gerlaine considered, "How awkward for your mother."

Moraunt shot a warning glance at his daughter. Gerlaine hadn't giggled but wasn't taking this seriously at all. Quickly he steered the contender toward the archway. Veluvius followed, unobtrusively measuring Brian with a practiced eye.

"I was right," he congratulated himself in a pleased whisper. "But then I always am. The extra large casket will do very nicely."

"Brian, my lad." Moraunt put a fatherly arm about the boy's shoulder. "The last time I saw your father, he was trying to put his sword through my skull. Do hope he's not still sulking over it. You must see our gardens. Let's show him our roses, Veluvius. We'll press some in gold . . . for his mother."

Brian paused to beam at Gerlaine. "Till our wedding, my lady."

"I can't wait."

With a last pitying glance at Morgan, Brian followed the king, Veluvius and Evan.

"I'll go prepare," Morgan decided. "Wish me luck, Gerlaine?"

"As if you need it with that thundering bore."

"You know, we could do away with all this nonsense if you'd just marry me."

"But not the war sure to follow."

"Prisoners of duty," The protest trailed after departing Morgan. "The same thing over and over. They come, you charm them. They propose and I dispose. Tedious . . . "

Dear Morgan. What a treasure he is, Gerlaine thought. Then she remembered the prophecy. "Lyonnais," she whispered, and there was strange new music in the sound, though it did remind her of a salad. She wondered just what he would look like. Brawny and brainless like the rest, no doubt. And yet there was something that stirred in her at the thought and the tantalizing words of the soothsayers.

"Is it true?" she asked of the walls. "Are you really coming, Lyonnais? Coming for *me* this time?"

We had a destiny once but it left

—

RUNNING HARD, LOWEN AND BRONNIE reached the open castle gates. Lowen anxiously scanned the road up from Tye; they weren't pursued. He dropped his knapsack and flopped down beside Bronnie, panting.

"I think . . . think we lost them. Hope Gwin got away."

"Never catch him. Gwin's too fast. We're safe." Bronnie sounded confident.

Lowen didn't. "Unless you decide to make a pot roast of the king. How could you be so careless?"

"It almost never worked before. I'm doing something wrong. Practiced for months, but honestly—"

"'Make me a pot roast'—and then she can't undo it."

"But what a moment! I mean, I'm really getting the fireworks down pat. You don't call down lightning like that every day." Not without the artist's ego, Bronnie relished the memory as she raised her hand and gestured at Lowen. "Remember? I just went ZAP!"

"Don't!" Lowen dove out of her lethal way and onto his feet. "You are all kinds of a hazard, fire, flood and domestic. Some magician!"

"I'm not a magician. I'm a witch! I did study with the Scottish women, and I was *very good* as far as I went."

Hungry and tired, Lowen felt anything but kindly. "If you were so good why didn't they keep you on?"

"I am a countess," Bronnie declared with dignity. "Witchcraft is only an avocation. Besides, it was all so dreary wandering around in the rain with flowers and thistles in my hair and my sinuses always stopped up."

"Oh, face it. You're a rank amateur."

With the same bruised dignity: "Of course I'm an amateur. Nobility can't take up a trade; it's simply not done."

"Nobility my noble, aching feet. Your father owns ten square miles of mud and a stone tower full of rats and bats. Countess, you have been nothing but trouble since Gwin and I asked your old dad for a night's lodging."

"You *had* to come." Bronnie's voice trembled on the verge of tears. "Father had to give you King Arthur's sword. It's all in the prophecy."

"He knew a fool when he saw one, but why did he have to saddle me with you?"

"He didn't have to. I—oh, Lowen, don't be angry with me. I'm scared and tired," She sniffled. "And I'm hungry, and I wish . . . "

The flood gates opened and Bronnie surrendered to a good honest cry. Lowen was instantly sorry. "Don't cry. Please don't."

The strangest thing, how uncomfortable it made him. Bronnie was unpredictable, sometimes maddening, but she could take the storm out of his worst anger with her first tear, and instead of a royal dressing down, Lowen found himself trying to buck her up. The three of them on the road for a year now, sometimes applauded and at others urged to leave rapidly through various misunderstandings due to his too-glib tongue or Bronnie's precarious command of her powers. But Lowen loved the road, a born performer. He loved drawing in the crowd, promising and often delivering wonders like Gwin's defiance of gravity, and Bronnie's uncanny eye for things to come. If he didn't love them, if they hadn't grown on him like extra limbs through nights when nobles threw gold to them or peasants threw aged vegetables, Lowen would have abandoned them and become something useful like a ratcatcher or wandering monk.

Always the road, always Bronnie with her repentant tears and that bloody-awful prophecy. Laughable: He had the sword. There it was, carefully wrapped away and tucked into the straps of his knapsack, but the rest of it, the bit about some princess and Morgan toppling before him? Come *on*, Bronnie.

Standing over the huddled lump of her, Lowen lifted his head to the stone castle that dominated the countryside, and for the second time that day became aware of an odd feeling like tiny spurts of energy in his chest, as if some force beyond him were determined to ignite the damp wood of his spirit. He'd felt it first when they trudged into Tye and saw Moraunt's castle towering above. Well—nonsense. Folderol. Bronnie'd had a good girl-cry. Time to cheer her up.

"Well now." He lifted her gently and wiped her cheeks with a ragged handkerchief. "Look on the good side. We've a command performance in the castle tonight. We'll earn enough to keep us for a month, eat till we burst, and sleep warm."

A last sniffle. "In the stable."

"You love horses. The stable's fine."

"No, it's not. Not for you. You're a prince and someday you'll be a king."

"Of what?"

"Lyonnais."

There she went again, that was her all over. For the hundredth time: "Bronnie. Countess Bronwen of Caermarthen, there isn't any Lyonnais anymore. It's gone. I'm the only prince in the world who came home to find his country gone out with the tide."

And so much else, so many blind fools, so many good, fine things learned and loved too late.

"It's better this way. This is all I'm good at. I can sing and make people laugh, but a king? I couldn't lead a dance around a may-pole. Tried it once and sprained an ankle, and as for that sword your father couldn't wait to palm off on me, you just watch me at the next pawn shop."

Bronnie was not to be swayed. "But the prophecy said 'He will lose the world and find himself.' That was written on the sword."

"It's not there now."

"Trust me."

"Well," he shrugged, "The losing part is right anyway. Look, I don't want to hear any more about prophecies, not a word. I'm a clown, not a king. Kings are brave and wise like . . . like my father. I've been the worst kind of fool for eighteen undistinguished years, and I am *very happy* this way. One more word about kings or destiny out of that foggy little head of yours and"—Lowen gave it up for pacing impatiently up and down before the gate. "Hurry up, Gwin. I'm hungry."

From the castle a great bell tolled twice.

"What's that?" Bronnie wondered.

"Dinner maybe?"

While the sound of the bell still rolled over the courtyard, the powerful voice boomed out: "THE SUN HAS SET!" Lowen and Bronnie leaped into each other's arms.

"WHERE IS HE WHO CHALLENGES MORGAN, THE KING'S CHAMPION?"

Lowen revised his guess. "It's not dinner."

"That? Don't let that fright you, ragamuffins." Prince Brian strode toward them, helmeted and clad in a long mail coat that shone with recent oiling, scabbard rattling at his side. "That would only be Sir Morgan, eager to die and roaring his last."

"Really?" Lowen peered up into the red face towering over him.

"Who's going to dispatch him?"

"Who?" Brian bellowed, regarding Lowen like something he might step on were he not bound in another direction. "Myself, that's who?"

"No offense, sir."

"Why?" Bronnie asked simply.

"Questions they ask: what's that and why? You should both ask less and wash more by the look of you—but 'tis my wedding day and myself in a fine mood, so I'll tell you. They've a foolish notion that before I can marry the Princess Gerlaine I have to deal with that great bag of wind who just pained my ears."

From Brian's sheer size, the outcome seemed a sure wager to Lowen. "Peace to his ashes."

Bronnie plied him: "Tell your fortune, sir?"

The war clouds vanished from Brian's florid countenance; he actually smiled. "And what kind of fortune could you tell, colleen?"

"The one that's coming for you. Only a penny."

"A bargain," Lowen assured him. "She's the best in the trade."

Brian inspected her doubtfully. "I'm thinking that's hard to swallow." Still, he produced a penny and gave it to her. "Here's my hand. Give it a bash."

Bronnie caught and held his gaze. "I don't read palms but faces. Eyes. Voices. Yes, there is a thing you search after, the one prize you seek above all other treasures."

"And surely I'll have it."

"Oh yes," Bronnie said, concentrating. "Very soon. Perhaps today you will find it."

For the first time in a short life not over-burdened with thought, Brian felt himself drawn toward and into something beyond him. "You . . . you have strange eyes, girl."

"They see."

With an effort Brian shook himself free of the sudden glamour. "Ah, it's fey you are. Be off now. The humor is on me to marry and there I'm bound." He turned and swaggered through the gates.

"Lots of luck," Lowen called in farewell. "You tell weird fortunes, Bronnie. No one ever understands them."

"Neither do I."

"So why tell them?"

"Because I see them. Like getting someone's else's letters you wouldn't want to read anyway."

"Then why can you never tell mine?"

Oddly, Bronnie ducked away from the question. "It doesn't always work. Yours is too far away. Or too close, I can't tell."

Lowen would have noted something about imperfect training, but pounding footsteps behind them made him turn..

"My lord!" Gwin threw himself down on the ground, gasping for wind. "Here I am."

"Stop calling me lord, it's dangerous. Did you get lost?"

"Lost," Gwin panted. "And chased and hit with stones and mud balls and mother knows what else, but here I am: Gwinnoc the Fox! Gwinnoc the Inspired. I led them after me so you could escape. Then I hid in a barrel, and where I hid I heard things, and what I heard made me think, and *what* I thought led to—by Excalibur, I'm so brilliant it hurts."

"This is historic," Bronnie declared. "Gwin has an idea."

"A FANTASTIC idea!" Gwin exploded. "Not a new dance, no new trick. Guess."

"A new song?" Bronnie ventured.

Gwin snapped his fingers at them "Poo. You're not even warm. Dear lord and countess, allow a faithful servant to observe that you haven't the brains of a cabbage between you. Listen. In my hiding place I heard two men talking, and I suddenly realized where we are."

"The Northern March," Lowen shrugged. "All that silly prophecy stuff. What else is new?"

"Right. Remember when we played in London, that old story-teller on the bill with us?"

Lowen remembered too well. "His act stunk."

"And ours was better?" A dark glance at Bronnie that remembered pot roasts and one more hasty exit. "He told the story of Gerlaine of the Northern March." Gwin swept a dramatic arm toward the castle above. "Well, this is the *place*. Remember in the story about Morgan?"

"Do we ever! A prince just went in to fight him."

"It's just like the story," Bronnie said. "They're deciding who's to marry the princess." She couldn't resist adding with sweet malice, "She's probably fat with buck teeth."

From the castle the great bell tolled three times with a finality that made funerals sound like Christmas. Lowen frowned at the tidings. "I think they've decided. Get to the point, Gwin. We've got a show to do."

"Oh dear." For a moment Gwin looked uncertain but drew himself up and struck a commanding pose. "We do not perform tonight. Not us, not as three raggedy-baggedy patch-pants actors. When we enter these gates tonight—"

"Make way there. Make way."

Gwin was pushed aside by the two courtiers, Evan ap Evan and Owain ap Gluyas, bearing between them a litter on which lay the suffering Brian of Ulster. His head was swathed in bandage, his torn mail coat liberally splashed with blood but covered with a lovely spray of roses.

"It's him," Lowen gaped. "The knight that—but he just went in."

"Two minutes is average," Evan stated briskly. "Business as usual."

"Morgan never dallies over these disputes," Owain explained. "This one's most fortunate. Morgan left him alive. Out of the way, if you please. Our guest has a boat to catch."

"Bronnie," Lowen muttered, "I feel sick."

"I'd give you two aspirin," she sympathized, "but they haven't been discovered yet."

"Anything for panic?"

"Sorry."

"Fortune girl," Brian implored feebly, "why did you lie to me?"

"But I didn't, my good lord. When I looked into your eyes, I saw a conceited fool."

"You lied. You said I'd find what I sought."

"You will," Bronnie promised. "You've been chasing your own death for years. Keep trying, you'll find it. Here." She placed Brian's penny among the roses. "Compliments of the management."

Brian went on groaning as the courtiers carted him away.

"So what's your great idea?" Bronnie pressed Gwin.

Looking after the ruin of Brian, Gwin wasn't sure this was quite the moment for revelation. "Tell you later."

"Tell us now," Lowen demanded. "Later we may not be here that long."

"Well, my lord . . . "

"Stop calling me that."

"I want you to know I've thought this out carefully. I have the greatest confidence in you. Those men in the market place were talking about the prophecy and mentioning you—I mean a certain prince of Lyonnais."

"What did I tell you?" Bronnie clapped her hands. "At last. It's all coming true. Oh, Lowen."

"Who carries the great sword Excalibur—"

"I told you, I told you," Bronnie yipped. "Oh, *Lowen*."

"And," Gwin concluded triumphantly, "who is destined to marry Princess Gerlaine."

Bronnie deflated. "Oh."

Gwin rushed through the last like the fine print on a contract. "After he has defeated Morgan."

"Oh, that's good," Lowen chuckled. "That's so lame it's laughable. Lyonnais lays out Morgan? You can't be serious."

"But I am."

Lowen laughed harder. "And they swallowed it?"

"Up to the hilt and wanting more. It's *prophecy*."

"That's rich, so it is." Lowen plunked himself down by his knapsack. "Prophets in this country can't even get the weather straight."

"This one did." Gwin knelt beside his master, both of them hooting together, in contrast to Bronnie who gazed gloomily at the castle, quite sure something in the prophecy had been lost in translation.

Lowen clutched at his heaving ribs, "And I suppose the king is just waiting to hand over his throne."

"Oh no . . . no." By now Gwin was laughing hard enough to bring on hiccups. "They're scared blue. They think he's come in secret with an army. They're going to keep Morgan up all night just waiting to kill him."

Lowen lay back and roared at the insanity. "B-big, bad Lyonnais . . ."

"Ten feet tall and mean as a bull with indigestion," Gwin capped it. "Oh, can't you just see their faces when I tell 'em it's you?"

"Oh, I can. I can just . . . " Caught up in the absurd joke, Lowen was a little slow on the uptake, but when Gwin's intention sank in, his laughter strangled into a wheeze. He rose dangerously. "When—you—what?"

Gwinnoc had never been at a loss for words. From Lowen's expression, he would now need his inspired best to escape violence. Meekly: "When I tell them it's you?"

Lowen's tone was the hovering quiet before a hurricane. "But you're not going to tell them, are you?"

"Master, how can we deny what's meant to be?"

"Because if Morgan doesn't dismember you, I will. You'll get me killed. You'll get us all killed. What d'you think they'll do when they know? Slap our wrists and send us to bed without supper?"

"My lord—"

"Don't *call* me that!"

"—your attitude is sacrilege."

"So is dying young! Maybe you think the king will just say 'Oh well, it's fate. Take my throne and my daughter. Take two, they're small.' It's not fate, Gwinny, it's politics, and when a king wants to stay on his throne, someone's head comes off. Not one word. Not—one."

"Why? Don't you want to be what you were born for?"

"Not if I have to die for it."

The force of it surprised Gwin but didn't blunt his argument. "What dying? You're a great swordsman. All you need is confidence, and that I have in you. Blood will tell."

"*What can it tell when it's all over the floor?*" "And what are you now?"

"A free artist and alive, that's what. Who needs a used prince?"

"Then do it for Bronnie and me," Gwin implored. "We had homes once. I had a position and pride."

"Said the born snob."

"Lady Bronwen was once a noble countess. What are we now, I ask you? What *are* we, Lowen?"

Lowen answered with a conviction equal to Gwin's. "We're actors."

"Ha! Call a ripe cheese a rose and it still stinks. I have the confidence in you that you lack, but blood will tell." Gwin dropped to his knees before Lowen, hands wringing his plea. "Prince, I beg you. By the moon, by the stars, your destiny is already happening all around you. All you have to do is let it."

"No, no, *no*." Lowen stormed away from him in frustration. "Can't you understand? I don't want to be a king. You need a destiny? Fine, take mine cheap. You with your great ideas, Bronnie with her prophecies, and Morgan in the castle waiting to—well, it's not me, friends. Being a king is . . . everything I'm not."

For a moment Gwin heard that strain of bitterness again and the strength under it that always haunted the edges of Lowen's flippant laughter. When he turned back to Gwin, it was himself pleading now.

"Kings are old news, always were, always will be, but us? Gwinny, we're something *new*. Bronnie always said to trust her visions. Half the time she's wrong as a left shoe on a right foot, but now and then she sees things I want to believe in and hears names no one's yet christened a child. Like Shakespeare and Milton."

"Go on," Gwin scoffed. "What self-respecting father would name a child 'Mil-ton'? It sounds like a weed. Who's he?"

"Bronnie doesn't understand it either: Some careless old man who'll get to be immortal for losing a paradise. And other names like Garrick and Kean, Olivier and some Welshman called Burton. They'll all come together in 'theatres'—and no, I don't know that word either, but they'll imagine and write and speak words that soar up like flame and live forever when kings matter no more than last year's weather.

"And we're the start, Gwin. Players like us, drifting from one palace or pigsty to the next with holes in our shoes. We're the founders of what those men will call tradition. And whoever sees us perhaps sees—just for a moment, maybe—something so much finer than kings because it touches them where they live. And they'll remember."

"*Oh shut up.*" Sitting unhappily apart from Lowen and his inspiration, Bronnie sprang up in a fury that tore her voice jagged. "Just shut up. You're stupid, stupid, stupid! And I hate you!"

Which she demonstrated by darting away in through the castle gates. Lowen stared after her, stunned by the outburst. "Go after her, Gwin. She's just tired and hungry."

In some matters Gwin was more intuitive than Lowen. "I think we should leave her alone."

"What's got into her all of a sudden? I mean, you and I were just talking."

"Maybe she's tired of sleeping in stables. I know I am."

"Gwin—enough. Like she says, shut up," Lowen growled.

"Yes, my lord." Gwin followed Bronnie into the courtyard. *Shut up he says, but there'll be our destiny one way or another, Lowen.*

The prince of nowhere on any current map thought to take up his bundle and make for the castle after them. His stomach rumbled, reminding Lowen of its needs, but instead he sat down again by his knapsack with the uncomfortable air of a man who wanted to believe himself right—he *did* lay it on a bit thick to Gwinny about futures—when now and then a clammy little voice hinted he just might be wrong.

His hand rested on the long, wrapped object strapped to his pack. Excalibur. Lowen brushed his fingers along the hidden blade. "The next pawn shop for you, troublemaker. Get me killed, you will."

And yet, as his hand slid along the concealing cloth, he felt again that tingling in his empty stomach, not hunger but a new and definitely odd excitement drawing him on against any conscious wish. Lowen shouldered the pack and stood gazing up at Moraunt's castle with mixed feelings.

"Who wants to live like a king? I just want to live."

As he started through the gates, the great ominous bell began to toll, shivering over Lowen like a funeral knell. "Ah, pack it in. Don't call us, we'll call you."

Dusk with roses

—

LOWEN PERCHED IN A CRENNEL OF THE CASTLE garden wall, picking at the remains of a chicken leg. In contrast to his earlier mood, there was a serenity to his expression now; he might have been counting stars or fireflies. The air was heavy with the scent of flowers being generous to the world before folding up for the night. He felt equally glad of a full meal and being away from Bronnie and Gwin for a brief but welcome change. They would perform before the court in an hour or so, sleep warm and dry, and tomorrow would take care of itself. Life was good.

"Your Highness! Princess Gerlaine, where are you?"

The voice booted Lowen out of meditation. The branches of a tree partly obscured his view, but as he looked, a slender girl came into view, and somehow, to Lowen, the fragrance of roses trebled with his sight of her. She appeared to be nursing an injury to her left hand.

"Here, Veluvius," she called. "In the garden."

Lowen was a clear-headed youth, but the sight of her gave him a distinctly peculiar sensation, like laughter and tears all mixed together. He was looking at a princess worthy of the title—and nothing in Lyonnais had ever looked as good. As for the lean, lunging courtier who bustled in, Lowen could read pomposity and self-importance in every line of the middle-aged minister, perhaps overlaid with terminal concern. Regarding Veluvius, Lowen failed to read as well the craft and danger.

"Your Highness." Veluvius planted himself before Gerlaine with a curt bow. "Urgent news. The soothsayers have sent further word."

"Again?" Gerlaine put the cut hand to her mouth. "It's been a busy day."

"The worst of days," Veluvius asserted. "The Prince of Lyonnais is said to be within our city walls. We have doubled the watch—such as it is."

"He came," Gerlaine murmured half to herself. "But he sent no word?"

"Ah no." Veluvius looked like a frustrated fox with a strong scent in his nose but no visible prey. "And no challenge sent to Morgan. I suspect treachery, Princess, possible an army crouching to attack. I *smell* it."

"Oh you always smell something. You were born old."

"I was not, lady, but government does that to the dedicated."

"Here we are in the garden in a lovely dusk with flowers working overtime to perfume the air, and—Veluvius, were you ever young enough to believe in magic or even fall in love?"

This was not what Veluvius needed to hear. Lyonnais was near, danger imminent, and a million things to be done immediately. "Yes. Princess," he countered waspishly. "I have also had measles and mumps but I outgrew them too."

Gerlaine sighed. "Pity."

"By your leave, lady." Veluvius started away. "A day of trouble, nothing but trouble." Another thought halted him; all was not gloom. "There *is* some lighter news, say rather irrelevant. There is a troupe of minstrels to perform tonight."

"Players?"

"Yes, my lady." Veluvius trailed distaste behind him. "At a time like this—actors! I vow I am cursed."

He was scarcely gone when the vibrant new voice startled Gerlaine. It was the kind of voice one listened to.

"'He that plays the king shall be welcome.'"

Gerlaine searched the garden for the disembodied voice. "Who said that?"

"Shakespeare said it. Or he will someday. Bronnie's never quite sure."

"Who are you," Gerlaine challenged. "For that matter, where are you?"

"One of the actors." Lowen hopped down from the wall and into Gerlaine's appreciative view. Before thinking at all, she definitely liked what she saw as he swept low in a graceful bow. "Yes, my lady. As that frightfully serious gentleman described—act-ors! My name is Lowen: singer and clown, fool enough to think me wise, wise enough to know I'm a fool. And my lady's servant."

Her father's perceptive daughter, Gerlaine doubted he was a fool. Something in his expression belied foolery beneath the panache. And it *was* a rather inviting face. "What brings you to the garden?"

"I was going to pick some flowers—oh, not the roses, just some of the wildflowers by the wall."

"You're welcome to them." Gerlaine wanted him to linger; on the other hand she mustn't allow familiarity, even though—how odd, she thought. *There's a weird feeling about all this, as if the evening and roses are drunk on their own perfume.*

Lowen suddenly seemed not to know what to do with his hands. "Ah—Bronnie's mad at me, don't know why. I thought some flowers would cheer her up."

"Bronnie. Is she your lady?"

"Absolutely not. She's my headache, my cross to bear. Princess, you have no idea. A half-trained magician is a lethal weapon."

Gerlaine didn't know quite how to respond to the piquant statement. Definitely not the sort of thing one heard every day. "Yes, I daresay."

This actor Lowen intrigued her; a mere commoner in dire need of tailoring but refreshingly different from the booming, sword-rattling princes she was forced to endure until Morgan removed the rubbish.

"Very dangerous." Feeling decidedly odd, Lowen suddenly needed to fill silence with conversation. "Once she threatened to turn me into a toadstool and I dared her and she went ZAP—"

Gerlaine couldn't help laughing. "And you were a toadstool?"

"No. When the smoke cleared, Gwin was a mushroom and it rained for a week."

"Oh, I'm glad you're playing tonight." Gerlaine giggled. "You are funny."

"A talent for that." Lowen bowed again. "If nothing else."

"Then take your lady some roses as a gift. We always give roses to our guests," she added with more truth than was apparent.

"Yes, I met one of them leaving."

"Oh, Prince Brian. Now there, Master Lowen, was a fool worthy of the name."

Lowen remembered bleakly. "Do they all go out that way?"

"Rules of policy." Gerlaine felt her answer lame as the policy itself. "But Brian was such a crashing bore."

"Colourfully awful," Lowen agreed. "But I can see why he came. I mean—" He stopped abruptly. "Did I say that?" Something was distinctly odd about this place and this meeting. If such was possible, he could almost *hear* the perfume of the flowers like a fine humming in the air or perhaps blood ringing an alarm in his ears. "Princess," he confessed, "I feel very strange."

"You look fine," Gerlaine assured him. "A little dusty perhaps but—quite fine."

As she gestured, Lowen noticed the blood. "You cut your hand."

"My garden shears, really nothing."

"Let me see." Lowen took her hand. "Just happen to have something for it." He drew a small phial from a pocket in his tunic. "Bronnie makes it out of herbs and cobwebs."

And less mentionable substances but no need to go into that. "For cuts and snakebite."

"There are no snakes here."

"'Course not. They're scared of this. Hold still, won't sting at all."

He daubed tincture on the cut, taking infinite care and far longer than needed.

"You have a gentle touch, Lowen." This close to him, Gerlaine noted other contradictions to this (she had to admit) fascinating player. "You don't look like a clown. More like—I don't know, but something else."

"No," Lowen denied with a vigorous head shake. "Just a clown born and bred."

"But it's nice to talk with you."

When Lowen allowed himself to meet her eyes, the queer feeling trebled, sheer excitement mixed with music. Time seemed frozen a moment too long; Gerlaine remembered herself. "May I have my hand back?"

"Your hand?" Lowen came out of a haze. "Oh. Yes. Of course. All done."

Gerlaine sensed their silences had been too long and pregnant, clearly needing safer conversation. "Do you—travel much?"

"All the time, my lady. Name the castle or town, we've played there."

"The court of Lyonnais?"

"Oh-h . . . once or twice. It's not—"

"—there any more, I know. But you've seen the royal family?"

"Yes. The king was a fine man."

Gerlaine couldn't resist the question. "And the prince?"

"Oh dear," Lowen laughed. "You mean that prophecy that's all over your market place: Lyonnais galumphing out of the west to do in Morgan and claim you. Curious, Princess?"

Feverishly, but that was her own business. "Not at all, just cautious," she answered coolly. "He may be leading an army against us."

Lowen hooted. "*Him?* That lump couldn't lead his grandmother to lunch."

"Oh, then you have seen him."

"He was . . . underfoot a lot. I heard all the stories by way of the kitchen. A clod, lady. They say he once bored the entire city of London.'

"Oh, really now!"

"Well, that might be a bit much, but he's not the sort to bother you. All he ever wanted was the fun of being a prince. The hunting and dancing, all play and as little work as possible, which is bad news for kings in failing health. They said physicians were ever coming to tend him. It was all over the court how scared the prince was, because he'd actually have to work at his title, so to speak. And how grave the king looked."

"All good kings look that way," Gerlaine agreed with authority. "It comes with the crown."

"Well, the whole country knew he was ill, and the sicker he got, the more scared his son became."

"Of what?" Gerlaine pressed.

"Some said one thing, some another. I think the boy was scared he wasn't good enough."

"Oh rot!" Gerlaine stamped her foot. "Devil all that. He should have just pitched in and tried his best."

"Well yes," Lowen considered. "That would have been the admirable thing to do, but he didn't. Played hooky and went hunting in Cornwall."

"That is disgraceful," said Gerlaine with conviction. "Bad form all around. What happened to the king?"

Lowen only shrugged. "Who knows? That great storm came up, broke through the sea walls and—zap. No more Lyonnais."

"How sad."

"For the country, yes, but no tears for the prince. He bloody well deserved it."

"But I am curious," Gerlaine confessed. "The prophecy, you know. What does he look like? Is he at all . . . presentable?"

Her question had an overtone of eagerness not lost on Lowen. A little imagination would not be amiss. "A toad," he assured her. "Well—in all fairness, praising him with faint damns, he was sickly as a child, a malady that cost much of his hair and complexion. When I saw him, he seemed a bit jaundiced. And there was that unfortunate wart on his nose that he never could rid himself of."

"Well, he could still be dangerous." Gerlaine tucked her shears in her belt. "Good or bad, a prince wandering about without a country could be just the sort to snatch one if he can. And if he's bald, he won't be hard to identify. I really want to take his measure."

"Oh, there goes that wheezy prophecy again and the sneaking suspicion you'll actually like each other."

"Rubbish," Gerlaine scoffed.

"Complete and utter."

Roses as courtesy to parting princes was a bit of a white fib, Gerlaine knew. Now she was conscious of a thumping lie. "You don't just see a perfect stranger and—"

"And just love them, no," Lowen finished, feeling a little dizzy. They were very close to each other, early stars twinkling in a velvet sky, the moon smiling over the garden wall, and the roses outdid themselves for perfume.

Gerlaine blurted: "Was he anything like you?" She blinked and stepped back, embarrassed and utterly confused. "Did I say that? Now *I* feel strange."

"I know. Like someone tickling your wishbone."

She didn't dare meet his eyes; he'd read too much plain there. "Where's my wishbone, Master Lowen?"

He didn't dare either. "Bronnie says it's where you hiccup."

"Definitely my wishbone."

Her closeness and the need to kiss her almost overpowered Lowen before caution caught him by the scruff of his neck. "No, lady, that's not it and this is not like me, and I think I'd better go. Forget Lyonnais. He'll never come for you or your kingdom, and be glad of it. He's a toad, and a toad is a toad, and all the prophecy from Scotland to Land's End wouldn't make him good enough for . . . for—"

"It wasn't him, Lowen."

"Don't be a fool."

That sudden, cutting tone in his voice was ice water in Gerlaine's eyes. She gasped. "How *dare* you speak so to me?"

"I don't know. Forgive me." Lowen was painfully aware of going several miles too far. "I didn't mean it, just came out that way. I'm not even sure this is me talking. Princess, there's something very weird going on in this garden. I am a pragmatic person, the leader of a troupe, a business, but . . . "

"But?" she prompted.

"But since I came here—on my word just to pick wildflowers—I want to laugh and cry all at once. I want to believe in fairy tales—"

Gerlaine was smiling at him now. "You mean you didn't ever?"

"You deserve better." Lowen didn't know how like his father he sounded and the destiny he ran from.

Then Gwin's voice calling him. "Lowen! Lo-o-wen."

Time for the performance. He bowed again, trying to imitate the awkwardness of a peasant, and failed. "They're calling me. I'd better go." He started away but Gerlaine's voice stopped him.

"One asks permission to take leave of me."

No, wrong, one mistake after the other. He had never asked leave of anyone save his father. He must be careful, else tonight in this wretched wrong place at the worst time, the world could crash down around his head and Bronnie's and Gwin's as well. He moved to Gerlaine and bowed again. "I forget what few manners I have. By your leave, Princess."

She didn't want him to leave at all. "Where—where will you go after this?"

"Doesn't matter. Just I should never have come here."

"But alas, you did, Master Lowen."

"Oh—bollocks!" There are times in any healthy man's life when he throws his heart like dice to the fates. Lowen surrendered, drew Gerlaine to him and kissed her. One could safely say she enjoyed it completely. Hurrying into the garden with Gwin, Bronnie did not. For a small woman, she still had the voice of a countess when inspired.

"LOWEN! PUT HER DOWN!"

Gerlaine disengaged herself with a reluctant sigh. "Is that Bronnie?"

"Who else? What is it, Gwin?"

"Princess, your servant. Lowen, the steward wants to see you about the performance tonight."

"Until this evening, lady." Lowen strode away with Gwin, ignoring the dangerous light in Bronnie's eye. Once out of sight, Gwin spun around and hugged Lowen.

"Fantastic! Doesn't even know who you are and she's already wild about you. We only have to announce you and we're *in*."

"No. N, O." Lowen halted. "Gwin," he reminded him in softly murderous tones, "what part of sudden death don't you understand?"

"But the prophecy!"

Lowen threw up his hands—"Sheesh!"—and strode away toward the castle.

"Well, what part of destiny don't you understand?" Gwin called after him. "Back there in the garden is your future, the girlest girl anyone ever saw."

He would have enlarged on the theme, but a seething Bronnie kicked him in the shins. "Ah, shut UP!"

"Ow. What'd I say?" Favoring his injury, Gwin limped after

Lowen, leaving Bronnie alone by the garden wall, miserable, prophetic and not at all happy in her gift.

"She'll want me to tell her fortune tonight, and I don't want to, because—" Bronnie gasped at the brutal attack on her senses. The vision was suddenly there, a vivid picture before her. She couldn't help crying out. "No! Lowen, watch out!"

He was down, fallen on the earth—

"Please, no." Bronnie shut her eyes tight and clamped both hands over her ears, but the vision only came brighter and more horrible.

Lowen down and the tall man standing over him, raising the sword—

The terror of it crumpled Bronnie to her knees while the horrid picture slowly faded. She felt as if she'd run a mile and only come to a dark place where she and Lowen were lost.

"They all want to see tomorrow, and why? Doesn't it come soon enough?"

Bronnie rose to her feet, tasting the bitterness in her mouth. "Fortunes for sale, my lords. See tomorrow before it's yesterday, and if you're burned—well, that's how lessons are learned, my friends."

Lowen fallen, the tall man lifting the blade to kill him. It will happen and I can't stop it.

She glared with hatred up at the castle where her love would die. "Murderers."

Time for the performance. Bronnie trudged reluctantly toward fate that somehow must not happen. As she went, three heads rose above the low stone wall, Veluvius and the two courtiers. "Clearly a troubled child. Conscience perhaps?"

"Very peculiar," Evan ap Evan agreed.

"Looked like a seizure," Owain ap Glyas noted. "Hope it wasn't the food. Supper was excellent."

"Extremely suspicious, these actors," Veluvius mused. "Look you, Lyonnais is rumored here already, the wise men swear he is here, yet these three players are the only strangers unaccounted for."

"King Moraunt requested them," Evan reminded him.

As he did most of the time, Veluvius looked supercilious. "Oh, ye of little perception. Spies can be anyone anywhere. Keep your eyes open. If they're spies for Lyonnais, I will know before the evening is out."

Owain could barely stand Veluvius on the minister's most benevolent day, but now he was insufferably superior. "And then?"

"Then," said Veluvius with audible relish, "we hang them."

Their heads sank again below the wall.

Some days even a prince shouldn't get out of bed

—

IF BRONNIE WERE NOT A SEASONED TROUPER she could not have given the dynamic performance Lowen considered her best in months. She danced smartly with Gwin, smoothly controlled his impossible tumbles and somersaults that drew gasps from the court, and it was she who paced the left foot-right foot routine to gales of laughter.

No one in the hall, least of all Lowen, knew her desperate energy was driven by fear. Within herself she fought the terror of that dark vision, what she knew would happen but what she somehow must not allow to be.

As the laughter and applause died down, Lowen stepped forward and bowed to King Moraunt. "Your Majesty, Princess, gentles all—this concludes our performance."

"No," Evan protested. "Give us another dance. Another song."

"We really ought to keep them here," Owain ap Glyas ventured. "You there: give us the left foot-right foot again."

"Oh really," Veluvius sniffed. "Rather trivial, I thought."

At a whispered word from Gerlaine, Morgan crossed to Lowen. "Fellow, the Princess Gerlaine would speak with you."

"Master Lowen." Gerlaine extended her hand to him. "I pray you—"

When their eyes met, Lowen held her hand a little too long to go unnoticed by miserable Bronnie, King Moraunt or Morgan. "I pray you . . . "

"Enough praying, daughter." Moraunt a-hemmed tactfully. "Get on with it."

"I'm told your Bronnie can foretell the future. We have had strange omens. Perhaps she can see where we could not."

"I protest, Princess," Veluvius broke in. "These are matters of state."

Gerlaine turned to Bronnie. "Can you prophecy, girl?"

Something feminine and instinctive passed between them; Bronnie read it too clearly. "Not today, Princess."

Dangerous sailing; Lowen jumped in. "Hardly the office of mere minstrels, my lady."

But this night Gerlaine marched to her own drum. "Then perhaps something simpler like my personal fortune. To know one might be to see the other."

"Lady, I must decline," Bronnie said. "I have given a performance and am very tired. I can't."

"And Your Highness hardly needs a defective fortune," Lowen prompted. "Believe me, Bronwen improves greatly with a good night's rest. And so we bid this fair company good night."

"Stay." Gerlaine rose and descended to Bronnie, her challenge plain. "Perhaps you find me harder to read than the fools in the street."

Her tone was not lost on Bronnie. "My lady, the fools in the street want simple things."

Gerlaine preferred to ignore the *touche*. "I see."

But not Morgan. "Watch your tongue, girl."

"Oh, what can one expect?" Veluvius was bored, irritated and, on what had been less than a stellar day, wanted only to go to bed. "Thieves, rogues and common players. Vagabonds."

Snap! Too much for Bronnie, miserable as she was, miserable as this whole day had been. And like Gerlaine, she was her father's daughter. "I am no vagabond, old man! My father is—"

"Anyone care for another song?" Lowen volunteered with a warning glance at Bronnie. But her outburst snagged on something in the king's memory.

"Why is that girl so familiar?" he mused to Veluvius. "I *have* seen the child somewhere before."

"Perhaps I can see your fortune, my lady," Bronnie offered. "To read it wisely is your office."

"Then approach and read my future if you can."

44

Gwin edged close to Lowen. "Now's our golden time," he whispered. "Let me announce you."

"You want to get me killed? That's Morgan over there, big as a house and every room sudden death."

"My lord," Gwin reproved, "I would hate to think you a coward."

"So would I, but actually it's a reverent regard for life. Especially mine. And Bronnie's," Lowen added meaningfully. "And yours, if you know what's good for the three of us."

"Princess," Bronnie declared, "in your hand, I read only long life and a happy reign as queen."

"With no king?"

"But in your eyes, I see very faintly a good man."

"Would it be Lyonnais?"

"I—can't tell, Lady."

"But close at hand?"

"Very close," Bronnie sighed, "though you may not know it."

All attention on Bronnie, no one noticed Gwin slip away and out of the hall.

Gerlaine tried to conceal her eagerness. "Can you see him more clearly now?"

Bronnie laboured to conceal something else. "I—I only see that he is a good man who cares more for you than your throne."

"Oh, excellent," Veluvius grumbled. "No political sense. A lot of help."

"I tell you, Veluvius," Moraunt was sure now. "I've seen that girl, but where was it?"

"Master Lowen," Gerlaine called cheerily, "your seer gives good fortunes. I should reward her. Tell me, girl: does he look like a king?"

Bronnie winced with the brutal clarity of her vision. "I see only that—that he will face danger for you very soon. I see him hurt, fallen."

She could bear it no longer. The dark force of what she saw wrenched at her small body. "And you, Princess—"

Bronnie broke off, twisting around to face the court. "And you and you and you all will make him risk his life for the vanity of one spoiled girl."

A general gasp of reaction as Bronnie stabbed a finger at the prime minister. "And your stupidity, Veluvius."

Lowen beseeched her. "Bronnie, be still!"

Veluvius gaped at her. "The wench is raving mad."

"No, not mad but sighted." It was too much for Bronnie to hold back. "The stupidity of dull old men who can't find a better way to rule a kingdom."

"Insolence" screeched Veluvius.

"Not at all," Gerlaine admired. "I've wanted to say that for years."

Moraunt rose suddenly. "Of course. I remember you now. Girl, your father rode with King Arthur. The Count of Caermarthen."

"Yes, old Caermarthen," Evan ap Evan remembered. "Heard he was dead. Never knew he had a daughter."

"My lords, this is absurd," Lowen pleaded. "She's no countess but a two-penny player like me. I found her in a rabbit trap."

This tweaked Evan's curiosity. "What the devil would she be doing there?"

"What else?" Owain saw that logic at least. "Waiting for a rabbit."

Veluvius keenly felt a need to return to the point. "I don't care if she *is* a rabbit. The little wench has insulted our whole court."

"By telling the truth," Gerlaine laughed. "Father, Veluvius, I know honesty is dangerous in statecraft, but can't we now and then indulge in private?"

"Girl, you will apologize," Veluvius demanded.

"That can wait," Moraunt ordered. "I want to know why the daughter of Caermarthen is travelling with common players."

"My lord," Lowen jumped in hastily, "Bronnie is exhausted. Prophecy always does that to her, and I really must get her to bed."

But the king's mind was quite made up. "I think not. Seize them!"

Led by too eager Morgan, the courtiers made a rush at Lowen and Bronnie—started at least, but the voice from beyond the hall froze everyone.

"ALL HAIL! ALL HAIL! MAKE WAY FOR LYONNAIS!"

"What's that?" Veluvius wondered.

Again the disembodied command, recognized by Lowen as Gwin doing a convincing Voice of Doom in the echoing corridor without.

46

More, if they lived at all through this evening, Gwin would hear about it for the rest of his subversive life.

"KNEEL AND HONOR HIS ROYAL HIGHNESS, THE PRINCE OF LYONNAIS!"

"It's him!" Gerlaine yipped for joy. "It's him. He's come. Oh, just plain—*goody!*"

King Moraunt was already moving. "Look to the guard."

As Morgan raced off for his sword, he vowed: "I'll murder him."

"I know." Lowen cringed inwardly, wishing he'd attended church more often or at least made generous donations. In the eye of a hovering hurricane, he snatched Bronnie out of the way of hurrying courtiers, royalty, shouted orders and total confusion.

Morgan reappeared, sword in hand. "I'm ready for him."

Evan and Owain dashed in from opposite entrances, crossing one another. "Alert the army," Evan blurted.

"What army?"

"Oh, sorry. I forgot." They disappeared again as the King and Veluvius hurried in, the prime minister sputtering commands. "To the walls."

"Odd. The guards say no one's there," Moraunt puzzled. "They can't see a thing from the walls."

"Impossible," Veluvius denied. "There's an *army* come against us."

—as Owain huffed back into the hall. "No, just the guards."

"But there must be an army," Moraunt insisted.

Yet again came the sound of Apocalypse. "ALL HAIL HIS ROYAL HIGHNESS, THE PRINCE OF LYONNAIS, KEEPER OF THE SWORD EXCALIBUR, UNDISPUTED HEIR TO THE THRONE OF BRITAIN!"

Thanks a lot, Gwin. Holding a trembling Bronnie, Lowen dismally pondered their life expectancy: at the outside, one day for the three of them.

Morgan stood with his sword, the picture of a hunting dog with a hundred scents torturing his nose and no quarry in sight. "I tell you I couldn't see anyone anywhere."

Off to one side, Gerlaine knew her own hour had come. "Fate. Blood. Romance and destiny. Ye Gods, what a day!"

"Never mind," Morgan growled. "He won't stay any longer than the last one—good lord, what's that?"

—as Gwin entered, brandishing aloft the great, shining sword. "Lords, ladies, His Royal Highness—AIEE."

He got no further as every man in the hall rushed at him. "Not me, you idiots!" With a flourish, Gwin stretched a proud hand toward Lowen. "Him."

A moment for the truth to sink in, then very slowly, all eyes swept back to Lowen. In the loaded silence, he managed a pathetic shrug. "Actually, I'm retired." Gerlaine swept across the hall to throw her arms around him. "Lowen!"

Morgan couldn't help himself. "Gerlaine, you stop that right now!"

He might as well try stopping a flood. "It's you, you magnificent liar, it's you."

As she kissed him soundly, only Owain remained sanguine. "Didn't know they were introduced."

King Moraunt was near shock. "Veluvius, tell me this is not happening."

"Your Majesty," Lowen attempted, "Bronwen and Gwinnoc are quite innocent. For myself, can't I just surrender now?"

Moraunt squinted at Lowen who did not improve with scrutiny. "*That* is Lyonnais?"

"Not much of a funeral, always hated ceremony. Perhaps a few flowers on the grave now and then."

"I knew it!" Veluvius crowed. "I suspected it from the first. These three hardly look like actors. Their backs are too straight and," a withering glance at Bronnie, "their manner toward their betters much too familiar."

"Oh rot," Gerlaine contradicted. "You thought they were common players."

Veluvius favored her with a vulpine smile. "I was being subtle."

"So." Moraunt moved to Lowen, struggling to reconcile disparate images. "You are Lyonnais."

"Not anymore. I'm retired."

"Boy, royalty doesn't retire; they just fall over. Where is your army? How close? How many?"

"I don't have an army," Lowen insisted. "I don't even have a country anymore."

"All the more reason to want one," Moraunt nailed the point home. "And what are you doing with the sword of Arthur?"

"Fellow." Morgan's tone was dangerous. "Have you trifled with the princess?"

"You could say that," Gerlaine confessed airily. "I'm going to marry him. Is there an army, Lowen? In the garden tonight I met a good, gentle man, a man I could trust and love all my life, but not as a conqueror."

"On my word, Gerlaine. There is no army."

"I want to believe you." Gerlaine meant it passionately. "I love you."

Blindsided by a girl and his own heart, Lowen felt an indigestible mix of joy, misery and a destiny downright perverse. "And I love you."

"Oh, I say." Evan couldn't contain himself. "Bad form."

"Rather," Owain agreed. "Should have spoken to her father first."

"I don't know how or why." And Lowen honestly did not. "But every road, every day of my life seems to have led me here. I was Lyonnais once, but the world needs a good clown more than a bad prince."

"I quite agree," Moraunt said, "but where did you get the sword?"

Bronnie spoke up proudly. "King Arthur left it in my father's keeping."

"Indeed?" Veluvius asked delicately. "May one ask for whom?"

"My father said a prince would come when I needed him."

"Some need," Lowen shrugged. "I pulled her out of a rabbit trap."

"Your destiny was etched on the blade, Lowen."

Evan inspected the sword wrested from Gwin. "Nothing there now."

"There was. Sad, strange runes of finding and losing."

"Then it's true, Father," Gerlaine announced. "I present the true Prince of Lyonnais and my intended husband."

"I'm ill," Veluvius knew. "I am positively ill."

"Father, I do think he qualifies."

"Are you out of your mind, daughter? Your late mother always boasted your intellect. Don't disappoint her memory or your loving father. Lyonnais, I can't believe you're here with no more entourage than two flea-ridden players. For the last time, and do consider your present condition, where is the army?"

"You hired me as an entertainer. What kind of an act did you think we do? Noah's Flood?"

"Oh dear," the king sighed. "All right, we'll start with him." At his gesture, Evan and Owain pushed Gwin before Moraunt.

"Don't worry, my lord," Gwin assured Lowen. "I have a high threshold of pain—OW!"

Owain twisted his arm hard. Gwin promptly fainted.

"That was not profitable at all," Moraunt gathered. "Try the girl."

"No!" Lowen exhorted the king: "You can't torture a girl."

"Oh, a brutal word," Veluvius explained, seizing Bronnie from behind. "In matters of state, we prefer the term 'enhanced persuasion'."

"Leave her alone," Lowen warned. "I mean it, old man."

"The army, girl. Where is it?" Veluvius twisted her arm viciously. As Bronnie cried out, Lowen dashed at the minister.

"I said leave her *alone*." He tore Veluvius from Bronnie so savagely that the man went sprawling. "It's all right, Bronnie. I won't let them hurt you."

The next instant Morgan had him helpless in tow, and Evan put a knife to Lowen's throat, quite eager. "Now, Sire?"

"For the last time, Lyonnais," Moraunt plied him. "The army?"

"I do not have an army." Lowen bit off each word. "As in zero, none." Suddenly he had the uneasy sensation that the voice coming from him was not his own. "And neither do you, my lord."

There was a moment of dangerous silence. Were he himself, Lowen might have discerned distant political thunder. "Anyone with half a brain can see that. If you had an army you wouldn't be dangling your daughter like a bone in front of hungry dogs, and if you had any notion of government, you wouldn't need to."

Lowen blinked at Bronnie, stunned as the rest of them. "Did I say that?"

In spite of their situation, she could smile. "I always knew you would someday."

Veluvius was deceptively casual. "Tell me. Have you . . . discussed this with anyone?"

"Who talks to actors? I don't want your country, and I sure as bloody hell don't want to fight Morgan."

The king looked reflectively to his one knight, in this case his salvation. "Oh, that's *right*. I forgot."

Like Moraunt, Veluvius saw the solution as absolute manna. "Precisely."

"It would be awkward hanging a prince."

"Not done at all."

"This way is neater and so beautifully legal."

Morgan bounded forward with a vindictive glare at Gerlaine. "I am more than ready, Sire."

Saving Gerlaine, the mood of the court relaxed, became even jolly. "More sporting this way," noted Evan ap Evan.

"Oh, quite," Owain was sure. "Give the chap a fighting chance, all that."

"Well now." Moraunt clapped one hand to the other: down to business as usual. "It seems we have a suitor for the princess. Sir Morgan, your gauntlet."

"Morgan, please don't," Gerlaine implored.

"Gerlaine, you force me. You mean to say you prefer this ridiculous excuse for a prince to a knight who has served you all his life?"

Gerlaine only dropped her eyes.

"Well, all I can say is, it's not very British!" Morgan punctuated the sentiment by hurling his heavy gauntlet onto Lowen's foot.

"Ow!" Wincing, Lowen picked it up. "This is a bit heavy. Do you have something in a light gray suede?"

"Don't joke," Gerlaine implored. "Morgan will mangle you."

"In his case for days," Morgan assured her.

"Gerlaine," Lowen said wearily, "my father used to say once you bleed on a white shirt nothing else matters."

Morgan flourished the gauntlet in Lowen's face. "At eight tomorrow morning, Lyonnais."

"I suppose I'll get flowers."

"Our very best," Veluvius promised. "Take them away."

"Wait!" Bronnie turned on Morgan, flinging back her arm. "Sir Morgan, you are a pot roast. And—ZAP!"

Ear-splitting thunder deafened everyone for a moment. Lightning crackled about the hall, but not much else. Morgan stood unscathed, but Gwin, just reviving, fell flat and lay still.

Lowen looked apologetically to Gerlaine. "I told you she was half trained."

At the moment Bronnie felt more absurd than endangered. "Well, I never get to practice."

She and Lowen were led away toward destiny. Evan and Owain carried Gwin.

Sort of redemption

—

LIKE ALL SELF-RESPECTING CASTLES, the Northern March had dungeons. Like all other castles, what they lacked in hygiene was made up in gloom. Evan ap Evan opened the rusty-hinged grate to one of them and prodded Lowen into it at pike point.

"Do you mind not pointing that thing at me?"

"Rules, don't y'know." A longtime civil servant, Evan always felt it safer to follow directives than think on his own. "After all, you're something of a menace."

Lowen's involuntary laugh had a hopeless sound. "I'm the only bloke around who doesn't want to kill someone, and *I'm* a menace?"

"Good job you can still laugh it off. It is a bit like a comedy, I suppose."

"Satire," Lowen defined "When you sit on a tack, that's comedy. When someone stabs you and you wonder why you're laughing as you die—that's satire."

Evan relaxed a mite, leaning on his pike. "Subtle, that's what you are, Lyonnais. Like your father, I heard. They say he charmed the britches off half the ambassadors in Britain without giving up enough land to plant a cabbage patch."

"It's called government. It's an art."

"Ruddy horse trading, I call it. Well—not much time," Evan judged. "Leave you alone to pray, what?" He paused at the entrance. Because the thought was new, it bothered Evan. "You could be right.

You've got to laugh sometimes when nothing makes sense. Stay serious, we'd all go round the bend, wouldn't we?"

The dungeon grate clanged shut on Lowen.

"Subtle," he smiled bitterly. "Father, there are so many kinds of fools. Which was I?"

Father, please get well. This is too much for me. I'm not big enough for your throne. I'll tell them what you said, but they won't listen, taught too long that to be a man needs the blood of a man on the point of your sword; they call that honor. You wonder why I laugh. But I'll tell them what you want.

Oh yes, I told them—

"My lords martial: my royal father has considered your petition that for the honor of Lyonnais we wage war against Cornwall. We revere your personal honor; unfortunately the bulk of our army is farmers who do not feel their honor stained by an absence of war but rather bolstered by their traditional role as providers. Besides, you are inconvenient just now as I've arranged to go hunting. Therefore—with your prudent reconsideration—my father will not go to war."

That was the flaw in me, Father. I couldn't tell, couldn't show them my concern for you and how you were slipping away. The little boy who can't believe his big, strong dad could leave him alone. I'll tell them what you said, but I don't like the slogans they're throwing at the commoners to make them think this is their fight too. They call it the war to end all wars. That's a bloody gem, that one. But I told them what you said, and oh, how they raged at that—

"Father, don't try to leave your bed. They're a pack of wild dogs not worth damning. They'll have their war because they want it, for the people to fight as they always do, with a bright red slogan, PEACE WITH HONOR' like blood on a child's face.—and I'll tell them for myself!

"Well played, Barons. You have convinced the people that your war is theirs. You know, though they don't, that Cornwall lies gutted by Irish raiders. King Mark could no more invade us than he could grow wings. But we ourselves admire your invention of—how did you put it?—a people's war, by which your peasants can go to bed with nothing and wake up with a mission to save the world and your new piece of Cornwall and new peasants to serve you.

"May I remind you that the season of storms is close at hand, and those men you would draw away to fight would be better employed at the sea-dikes. The sea, not Cornwall, is waiting to pour over our country."

They called me coward and slacker for that.

"Let me be plain. There's a man dying upstairs with his heart burned out from keeping your peace, and you weren't worth it. You can go to hell and I'll go hunting—"

And Gwin was with me when we tried to return, but there was nothing but wreckage and mud. One moment of despair, of giving up, and I lost it all.

"Gwin . . . GWIN." Lowen came out of painful memories and opened his eyes on the damp walls of the dungeon. He sank back on the cold stone ledge. "Father, I tried. I told them what you said. But till the day I can understand why they hated you and you still cared for them, I'd rather be a clown. How ridiculous, how downright wasteful to seed in me so keen an ability to ever measure the distance between the Ideal and the Actual. Laugh?" he asked of the bleak stones overhead.

"All right. No laugh."

Astonishing, Lowen thought, how clearly a man can think just before he dies.

CRASH!

The splintering of crockery screamed off the walls of the small antechamber. There was a problem. Necessity demanded the tidy elimination of Lowen and his confederates, though the decision was not unopposed, as the castle servants heard; in fact houses nearest the walls heard the smashing of plates that punctuated the blistering opinion of Princess Gerlaine as she cast her pungent vote.

BANG!

"Gerlaine—now Gerlaine, be reasonable," Morgan pleaded.

"You can take your bleeding reasons and—"

CRASH!

Then Veluvius: "Your Highness, I am appalled at your language."

"Not yet you're not, you mummified moron. I'm just getting started!"

Interesting to note fine points of policy. Moraunt's government was no more than that of the world in miniature, past, present and likely future. Lowen must die: that was politics. And legally: that was policy. Most of all for the good of their country: *that* was patriotism, and what heart would not swell with pride to the skirl of that tune?

"Daughter," Moraunt lectured patiently, "we do not do this sort of thing for pleasure. His execution—rather his defeat—at Morgan's hand is based on sound political thinking."

"Is it then?" Gerlaine seethed. "It's hard enough to make myself believe that you three could conceive that Lowen has an army anywhere. On the marginal chance that he does, I tell you flatly, he's got no local competition. What's more, I *love him.*"

"Nonsense, child. Pay attention while I complete your education. The guidance of a kingdom requires a special dedication that can forge a working tool from charity and politics, noble principles and occasionally—"

"Only when needed," Veluvius prompted.

"—regrettable but necessary mayhem."

Gerlaine caught her father up scornfully. "Right. As in the slaughter of the innocents."

"Bluntly put, but in your unvarnished vein, for the good of your country, Lyonnais gets rigor mortis."

"And we will have peace," Veluvius said, as if explaining day and night to a child.

"Poppycock!" Gerlaine stamped her foot in frustration. "Veluvius, you pompous, thumping bore. In sixteen years of watching supposedly wiser heads rule a state, I have time and again seen you fall on your aspirations. Oh, Lowen's got your number right enough. What's more, I love him and I always will."

Her father winced. "Please. Not again."

"A closed mind," Veluvius sighed. "Princess, you don't know what a chore it is to send all these princes, as it were, *pace requiescat.*"

Morgan, suffering his private pain, agreed. "*Dona eis requiem.*"

"Right again," Gerlaine snapped. "Translation: we've got to get rid of them."

Morgan's mind was not quick as Gerlaine's. In this moment he fell back on innate conservatism. "Is it so much to ask for peace in our time?"

"Oh, my poor dear Morgan," Gerlaine pitied. "Granite muscles and granite mind. Can't you see they're using you? You asked me how I could prefer Lowen to you. Simply put, he's a man with more on his mind than his hat. That's why I love him, and I would rather die than—"

"ALL RIGHT!" Morgan hovered, determined and helpless in the same breath. "All right, I heard you. You love him. You don't have to *run it into the ground.*"

Embarrassed by his outburst, Morgan bowed stiffly to Moraunt. "Your Majesty, I—I'll go arm myself."

As Morgan retreated, the king wondered, "What's got under his helmet?"

"Can't say," Veluvius confessed, equally at a loss. "Serious chap, young Morgan."

"Well, to get on with it." Moraunt converged on Gerlaine with Veluvius "For the good of the country."

"Just you wait," she promised.

"*Pro patria et gloria,*" Veluvius intoned piously.

"You'll pay for this, Father."

"Oh, I daresay not." Moraunt led her out. "Besides, if we're wrong, we can always apologize."

Lowen hunched on the chill stone bench in his cell. Beyond the walls he could hear preparations for the combat and, ultimately, his demise and departure accompanied by roses. On the lichened wall before him, a large spider caught and ingested a smaller insect. Lowen empathized with the loser. "I know how you feel."

Lowen?

He raised his head, startled. No one was at the grate. "Bronnie?"

It's me, the disembodied voice assured him.

"Where? I can't see you."

Here with you—well, sort of. The week we studied materialization I had a bad cold. Couldn't get out of bed at all, let alone study.

"That's my Bronnie, always good for half an enchantment."

No matter what anyone says, your name was on the sword.

"Right-o. Anyone for a fast game of destiny? At least a hand when I get killed? What, no laugh?"

No one's laughing anymore, Lowen.

"Why not. We've come to a place where it's all fate, prophecy and stupid tradition, the bloodier the better, and common sense begs at the door. I have to laugh or go mad."

No, Lowen. I'm going to get us out of here.

That was worth a sour grin. "Lots of luck. Now would be a good time. That's it, I guess. Fate or luck, it's happened, and what do I do? I ruin whatever chance we had the moment I saw you cry."

You always protected me, always there to help.

"Tell me about it. Pulling you out of that stupid rabbit trap, pulling splinters out of your foot. Wiping your nose, fixing your bruises, covering you up when you needed a nap—not that I minded, Bronnie, I really didn't. You were always the best part of the act. But Gerlaine . . . Gerlaine was different. She made me want to go back to everything I never could be and try to make it true all in a single day. There's a laugh in that somewhere if I could find it.

"All in a single day. Like that old song, Bronnie; you know the one—
"I asked of the bright morning
No more promise than a rainbow gives.
But I asked of the noontime,
Where does my true love live?
How does it go? I've forgotten?"

Bronnie's voice prompted surely—

The day ran before me, Run swiftly, your love is near.
Follow the sunlight, hurry the day,
Follow the song your heart can hear.
Come evening she'll be gone away.
Run swiftly, your love is near.

"That's more than I remember," Lowen murmured, "except that foolish heartsong I did follow."

I've never forgotten, Lowen. I can't.

"How did the ending go?"

I found in the evening
No more promise than tomorrow's dawn,
For I found in the evening
Only dark for my love had gone.
Lonely dark, for my love has gone.
"And the last of it," Lowen half remembered. "'Swift as a dream' . . . something like that?"

Beyond the walls of his cell the great bell tolled as it had for Brian, and a deep voice summoned Lowen to his hour. "Bring forth Lyonnais!"

He rose as a guard approached to unbar the grate. "Yes, it did go something like that."

Yet as he walked between the guards, Bronnie's voice followed him.
Swift as a dream runs out little day.
Brief is the song that fills our ear,
And autumn blows the leaves away—
Fool, oh fool, your love was here today.
Oh . . . fool, your love was here.
I won't let it happen, Lowen, she promised. *I just can't,*
"Any notion how?" Lowen asked the empty air. "Now would be very good for one of your best."

I'll think of something. I hear them coming, bringing you here.

A fine time for Bronnie to nap, Gwen thought, but just then she opened her eyes, sat up and spoke. "They're coming."

The grate groaned open. Owain ap Glyas entered, bearing the sword Excalibur which he laid by, He favored Bronnie and Gwin with a pitying glance. "Always they come and go." He shook his head. "Always the same."

"This Morgan," Gwin inquired. "Does he really eat nails?"

"Oh hardly. Strong though. Never defeated."

"And he's beaten twenty-one princes?"

"Twenty-two counting yours. Fast, good footwork, that sort of thing. Very efficient."

"I see." Gwin saw far too clearly, as Lowen came into view prodded on by a guard who unlocked the grate and pushed Lowen inside.

He had been granted a heavy and quite impressive coat of mail that fell below the knee, the skirt slit for freedom of movement.

"Showtime, Master?" Gwin asked.

"I guess so." Lowen surveyed his armor like something barely familiar. "Many a day since I wore one of these. Uncomfortable things."

Studying his appearance, Bronnie shook her head. "It doesn't suit you; somehow I thought it would."

"Just something I threw on for the occasion. Nothing formal but good enough to be buried in." Lowen shot a purposeful glance at the bored guard yawning beyond the grate. He lowered his voice, drawing Bronnie and Gwin to him. "Listen, you two. When the show starts, nobody'll be noticing you. Stay on the sidelines. When you see a chance, get out of here."

"There's no chance and you know it," Bronnie was sure. "If you lose, so do we."

"Too true," Gwen agreed. "Dear friends, this concludes our farewell performance—well, it's quicker than starving."

"I won't leave you, Lowen." Bronnie's steely determination struck him for a moment before her smile broke through like sunlight. "Why break up the act now?"

Lowen winked at her. "For all my shortcomings?"

"For all, Your Highness." Bronnie took an ancient locket from her neck and caught it about Lowen's, "Here. Wear this."

"Is it magic?"

"It's either for good luck or hay fever, I've forgotten."

"Nothing stronger?"

"Sorry."

"Well, if I start to sneeze, I'm covered." Lowen laughed suddenly at the memory. "Remember the time Gwin had a bad cold and had to do the show anyway?"

Bronnie remembered. "And he could hardly dance for sneezing."

"And the house thought it was part of the act. The *hand* I got!" Gwin's eyes went wide with inspiration. "What an idea!"

Lowen glanced uneasily at the guard. "Marvelous. I'm about to die and *now* you feel creative?"

"It's a great idea, my lord. A sneeze dance—look." Gwin flowed away from them into an intricate series of steps. "Step-two-three-AH-CHOO!" Flowing into a graceful somersault. "And-step-two-three—KERCHUNK!"

"Beautiful." Lowen applauded. "And you wanted to be a servant. You're a showman, Gwinny. That's what you'll be till the day you—" Lowen broke off rather than comment on the imminent. There was a gloomy silence. Gwin broke it.

"Must you remind me?"

"Just a thought in case you and Bronnie ever get out of here. There are days when even a prince can't make a penny," Lowen allowed. "I do regret I have only one life to lose for Lyonnais. Unfortunately it's this one." He gathered Bronnie and Gwin into his arms and tried to smile. "But we were a great act."

The entire court emerged from the castle into the bailey yard. Moraunt led the grim procession, followed by Morgan and Gerlaine who conveyed the impression of wanting to be anywhere but here and as distant from Morgan as possible. Veluvius followed with Evan ap Evan and Owain ap Glyas, each bearing the combat swords. Lastly Lowen, Bronnie and Gwin under guard. The morning sun shone gloriously to the accompaniment of birdsong as the procession halted.

Lowen breathed deep. "At least they've given me a lovely morning for it."

"Oh, I say." Owain admired. "Appreciating beauty in the face of death. Good show, Lyonnais."

"Look at all that iron on Morgan," Gwin whispered to Bronnie. His expression sharpened to purpose. "Quick: can you make it rain?"

"What'll that do?"

"I don't know. Maybe we could rust him to death."

"Lyonnais," Veluvius summoned him. "Are you ready?"

Gwin looked to Lowen and shook his hand. "Ready, Master?"

"Are you serious?"

"Then let's do this in style," Gwin decided. "We're still a great act; we'll deliver a great finish. The old insult routine."

Lowen reluctantly moved away to face Morgan, Gwin following as squire to take Excalibur from Owain.

"Prince Lowen of Lyonnais stands ready," Gwin proclaimed formally, "to meet with—uh—what's that fellow's name again?"

"Morgan," Veluvius snapped. "Get on with it."

"Oh yes. Morgan. An opponent of merely local repute—"

Morgan eyed Gwin dangerously. "Insults will go hard with you, boy."

"No offense, sir, not at all. But in Lyonnais *we* have never heard of you. Nevertheless my lord is ready to meet this Morgan for the hand of the princess—uh—Her Highness there."

With elaborate care, Gwin scrutinized every inch of the magnificent sword, pommel to hilt and along the blade. He ran a finger along the length. With a reproachful frown at Veluvius, he showed the sword to Lowen who drew a finger along the blade, inspected his find and meticulously transferred the result to Gwin who showed the accusing finger to Veluvius.

"Dust." He tested the edge with a dubious thumb.

Veluvius assured him waspishly, "We did sharpen it."

"Well—you tried," Gwin condescended. "One can't expect professional work in the provinces, but we will let it pass." With a graceful pivot, Gwin knelt before Lowen, Excalibur offered over one arm. "My lord."

"Lyonnais," Moraunt inquired with strained patience. "We do hope you're ready now."

"I suppose so." Lowen shrugged. "But couldn't we decide this with a stiff game of chess?"

Evan's eyes lighted up. "Oh, do you play?"

"Very well, and I have a wicked endgame."

"Alas, Sir Morgan does not," Moraunt informed him. "Veluvius?"

The prime minister stepped forward. "My lords, the rules of combat. If a weapon is dropped, there will be no replacement. If one or the other falls, no quarter will be given. To the death."

"For the last time," Gerlaine implored Morgan, "I plead with you. I *beg* you not to do this."

Morgan's face betrayed a riot of conflicting emotions—love, jealously, anger—

"You were always my friend, Morgan."

—and finally resolution. "It means so much to you?"

"It does."

His back stiffened visibly. "Sorry, Your Highness. Rules of chivalry. Ready, Sire." He took the sword offered by Evan.

"Lowen," Bronnie promised. "I'll be right here."

He tried to smile at her. "Remember the day I found you in the rabbit trap?"

"How could I forget?"

"Always meant to ask; what were you *doing* there anyway?"

Her answer was too soft. Lowen wasn't sure he heard it right. "I saw you coming."

At a sign from King Moraunt, a trumpet blared on the walls. "All move back. Give them fighting space."

The court and prisoners moved away in a wide circle about Lowen and Morgan. "My lords." Veluvius raised his arm and dropped it. "Begin."

Lowen and Morgan circled each other slowly, on guard, Morgan seeking an opening. For an instant he saw Lowen's guard lower slightly and flashed forward in attack. His blade whipped over, under and through faster than the eye could follow, and Lowen realized that not superior strength but speed, coordination and footwork were why Morgan was undefeated. The heavy sword was a mere streak of light in his hands, his feet those of a dancer.

On the other hand, superbly conditioned as he was, Morgan did not have the lithe body of a performer used to constant movement and even acrobatics. On the downside actors didn't eat that regularly. Morgan had 20 lethal pounds on Lowen, a difference eventually bound to tell.

But fleet as he was, Morgan's every blow was parried or missed completely; Lowen was simply not there to be hit. He knew Lyonnais was frightened—most men would be—but Morgan began to feel off his best form. He disengaged and circled again; never mind, he'd finish the man sure on the next attack.

A spattering of applause from the king and court. "Excellent defense, Lyonnais," Evan called before remarking to Owain, "Might as well say it now before he dies."

"Yes, longer than usual this time."

"But sooner or later."

Owain sighed at the inevitable. "What else?"

Morgan streaked in again with an overhand feint turning into a lateral chop that battered Excalibur out of Lowen's hands. Disarmed, he felt and heard the *swoosh!* as he leaped barely out of range. Morgan stalked him, ready to end it.

"Do something, Gwin," Bronnie wailed. "He's helpless."

No more helpless than Gwin felt. "What can I do? You're the magician."

Bronnie's eyes narrowed: desperate times required desperate expedients. "Pot roast." She wound up and flung her hand at Morgan. "ZAP!"

As with most times, nothing happened.

"Zap what?" Gwin wondered. "I wish you'd practice more."

"Shut up, I'm trying. Spirits of the fen, spirits of the woad, take this Morgan and make him a toad. ZAP!"

A clap of thunder tore out of the otherwise untroubled sky. Everyone looked up, but nothing else followed. Gwin was not surprised. "Bronnie, you're not even warm."

Safe to say that without a weapon and Morgan intent on mayhem, Lowen felt rather naked. By now he knew he had an edge for speed, but barely, and only that could save him. When Morgan caught one foot against the other and stumbled slightly, Lowen dove for his sword and grasped it, cat-quick on his feet again. Morgan aimed a vertical chop that ripped through Lowen's mail.. Once more they disengaged and circled. But Bronnie was a long mile from giving up.

"Come, weird sisters, come, I insist. Take this Morgan and turn him into mist. ZAP!" A sheet of heat lightning whitened the sunlit sky and rumbled away in thunder.

"Not it, Bronnie," Gwin hissed at her. "You're giving us weather."

"That one always worked—well, mostly."

"Good form, that Lyonnais," Owain commented. "Wager he goes another two minutes?"

"Can't." Evan shook his head. "Impossible. Im-bloody-possible!"

"Oh? Ten shillings on it?"

"Done. Shouldn't take your money, but I will."

Lowen had eluded him longer than any other opponent, and all the court were aware of it, the courtiers even complimenting Lyonnais on his speed and agility. By now Morgan knew that only a clever trick would save his reputation. Lyonnais was quite at home with a sword, and his body bent and sprang look wood of oiled yew. Yet— somehow Morgan couldn't like what he had to do, didn't like it at all. Once more he attacked overhand. When Lowen parried, Morgan locked hilts with the other sword, slid in and tripped him up, toppling Lowen to the ground.

Even as Morgan raised his sword, Bronnie darted forward to stop what must not happen. Gerlaine saw all of it in an instant, crying out even as Veluvius barked the command. "Strike, Morgan!"

"Morgan, don't!"

But Morgan had oddly hesitated a moment. As he swung his blade, Bronnie streaked between him and Lowen, catching the blow across her small body. The court gasped as she crumpled into Lowen's arms. Dead silence: Morgan stepped back and dropped his blade like something unclean. Lowen took up Bronnie's limp form like a broken doll and carried her to Gwin who could barely speak.

"My good lord, I—"

Gently, Lowen laid Bronnie at Gwin's feet, his expression hard to read. He stood for a moment, stunned. Veluvius broke the silence, sputtering. "Sir Morgan, why did you not strike? This is against knighthood, against—watch out!"

Only Gwin heard the low sound out of Lowen as he spun like a dancer and launched himself at Morgan. Unprepared and unarmed, Morgan could barely raise his arms before Lowen's fist drove into his stomach, forcing an undignified *oof!* from the king's champion. Morgan doubled over but Lowen snatched him erect and laid him to rest with an anachronistic but very efficient right to the jaw.

Evan was shocked at the dishonor. "Oh, I say. Unfair, foul!"

"Is it ever!" cried ecstatic Gerlaine as Gwin hurried to count over the fallen favorite.

"Time, my lords. One-two-three—"

Lowen only turned away, weeping, and went to kneel by Bronnie, as Gwin's arm tolled the last moments of Morgan's career. "Four-five-six—"

"I'm frightened." Gerlaine went to kneel by inert Morgan, patting his cheeks. "Morgan, wake up."

"Nine-ten." Gwin spread his arms like the angel of death over the vanquished. "He's out!"

"No wager," Evan denied to Owain. "Won on a foul."

"Glad to agree." Owain inspected the unmoving Morgan. "Bare-hand fighting: think it'll ever catch on?"

"Oh hardly. Much too violent."

Gerlaine was concerned. "Is he badly hurt, Gwinnoc?"

"Just a short nap, my lady. See even now where he stirs and rises like Phoenix from his own ashes."

Morgan opened his eyes and tried to focus on the cherished image of Gerlaine. "What hit me?"

"Fate, my dear. Are you all right?"

"Oh," he lied gallantly, "never better."

"I cannot understand this, Sir Morgan," Veluvius fumed. "Why did you not finish him? You had every opportunity." He picked up Morgan's sword. "I have a keen eye for these matters. Twice, even thrice this blade touched him. I—" Veluvius squinted closely at the blade where his answer lay. "There's no edge to it."

To Moraunt, this was just one more upset in a day that should have been canceled at dawn. "No edge?"

Veluvius presented it to him. "Dull as a butter knife."

"*That's* why I'm not dead?" Bronnie sat up and slid conveniently into Lowen's arms to a resounding HOORAY! out of Gwin. "I've been lying here thinking death can't be this easy and why aren't I bleeding profusely. Knocked the wind out of me, that's all."

"What a fool trick!"

"Oh?" She smiled invitingly at Lowen. "I thought it rather heroic. Come here."

"By St. Genesius, I can't take my eye off you for a minute. I ought to flat out give you the spanking of your irresponsible life. I ought to—"

"Ahh—shut up." Whatever Lowen ought never got spoken as Bronnie silenced him soundly with a kiss.

King Moraunt had gone many days, even months with a monotonous lack of surprises. This was not one of them. "Morgan? No edge to your sword?"

The guilty could only hang his head. "I couldn't."

Gerlaine said it with great tenderness. "Thank you, Morgan."

"Princess, I have been beaten. I beg you not to look at my shame."

"Oh stuff. Somehow it makes you more human. And very attractive."

To Morgan this was a new note in a girl he thought he knew thoroughly. "What?"

"That you couldn't do anything to hurt me." Gerlaine surrendered to giggles. "Oh, my wonderful Morgan: heart of gold, jaw of glass. I guess I've gotten used to you."

Moraunt was far from appeased. "Before I go all warm and treacly, Morgan—why?"

Gerlaine took her knight's arm. "Oh, Father, can't you understand?"

"Not in the near future, but believe me, I will try."

Lowen offered his hand. "Thank you, Morgan."

"My pleasure," Morgan returned, not without effort. "I think."

"Well, rules are rules, bargains are bargains." Moraunt bowed to destiny, no matter how .appalling. "You've won, Lyonnais. Gerlaine, do you accept him?"

A very self-possessed girl, at the moment she honestly didn't know. "I was so sure tonight. Now I'm confused."

"We both were." Lowen winked at her. "Welcome to the world, Your Highness. I think we both know who we are now. You're not foolish enough to marry me."

No part of a fool but still honest. "I almost wish I were—but no. And you?"

"As you said."

"You'd look so uncomfortable on a throne."

"Alas, and you can't dance."

"Or do spectacular but unreliable magic. Pity."

From a bleak vision of future chaos, King Moraunt now saw sunlight and rescue worthy of legend. "What, not staying, Lyonnais? What a shame after all this bother. Don't let us detain you."

Lowen took Excalibur from Veluvius—"May I?"—and presented it to Morgan. "I think you and Gerlaine will have the sense to use this very well."

Veluvius gasped. "You're just giving it *away?*"

"Only fair," Gerlaine reasoned. "Morgan and I ought to win something today."

Veluvius could not comprehend an act of clear political suicide. "He's mad."

"Quite often," Gwin agreed.

"In all my years as a minister . . . the prophecy clearly—"

"Forget prophecy," Lowen advised. "Bet on people."

"Was the prophecy so wrong, Lowen?" Gerlaine asked. "We met, Morgan fell, we lost each other and found what we really are."

"And really want," Lowen finished her thought.

"Thank you for the lesson." Gerlaine's very fond smile was mixed with a fugitive element of loss. "Farewell, Your Highness."

"Princess." Lowen bowed to her. Gerlaine's fingers trailed lingeringly over his cheek before she turned briskly to business.

"Come, Evan and Owain, let's see to Morgan."

"No, really," he protested, "I'm quite all right."

"Now, now. I want to count your teeth. Quickly, gentlemen, quickly. He won't break."

Lowen looked after Gerlaine as she shepherded the vanquished champion into the castle. He couldn't be angry at Bronnie or Gwin. Each had wished him toward what he never wanted or could be. Perhaps now with their lives staked and won by a hair, Bronnie and Gwin finally knew what they were born for. Lowen bowed to King Moraunt. "Sire, may we go now that the fate of nations is out of my hands?"

"By all means," Veluvius urged. "They confuse everything."

"You have our leave, Lyonnais, and swiftly if you will. I don't know if you're utterly mad or very sane . . . but thank you for showing me what a daughter I have." Moraunt's eyes followed Gerlaine as she disappeared into the castle. "I sometimes doubt if there is anything a father knows for sure. Come, Veluvius."

Officious to the end, the prime minister waved them off grandly. "You have royal permission to—oh, just go away, the lot of you." He followed after Moraunt and the guards, mumbling. "This was not my day. I knew it at sunrise."

"Help me out of this silly iron." With Gwin unbuckling him, Lowen dropped the mail coat on the ground. "So much for royalty and mayhem. Ready to go?"

"Absolutely," Bronnie answered.

"And do we all know who we are?"

"Players," Gwin shrugged. "Better or worse, that's what we are."

"Say it with majesty, man. The founders of the British stage tradition."

"Right." Bronnie took Lowen's hand. "And who do you belong to, cleave to and infinitely adore?"

"You, idiot."

"And who does Gwin belong to?"

"Us."

Gwin gave in to destiny at last. "Well, back to the road."

"The road needs us, Gwinny boyo. The world needs us. For when it gets too thick to see where it's going or too solemn to laugh at itself. Oh, there! I just remembered a great idea while I was dodging Morgan."

"And I was dying of fright," Gwin confessed. "A good idea?"

"A fan-*tabulous* idea! A new routine. We both come on with big wooden paddles that clack, see? We'll call them slapsticks. And I chase you—"

"ZAP!" Bronnie was carving strange figures in the air with fingers and wrist"ZAP!"

Gwin sighed. "*Now* she wants to practice?"

But Bronnie was not to be denied. "Just remembered what I've been doing wrong. It's all in the wrist. Watch."

"Don't!"

"Look out!" Lowen dove for the ground with Gwin a close second.

"Don't stop me." As if Bronnie could be stopped. "I've got it now."

She wound up impressively and flung her wrist at infinity. "YOU ARE A POT ROAST. ZAP!"

What followed dwarfed anything before. A bolt of lightning lanced at the castle, followed by ear-splitting thunder, blaring trumpets from nowhere, a booming of drums and jangling chords of music someone might later ascribe to Stravinsky. Then ominous silence and a heavy smell of ozone.

Lowen raised his head warily. "Who's a pot roast?"

"Just practice," she said. "Sort of to whom it may concern."

Apparently a number of folk were concerned . Loud dismay echoed from the castle and spilled out into the bailey yard. Evan ap Evan burst out of the lower level carrying a large covered pot. "Ye gods!" He panted up to Bronnie. "Veluuvius is a pot roast. You girl, you did this. Bring him back instantly."

"Of course," Bronnie temporized. "You'd better stand back. This can be hazardous."

Indeed, Evan realized his proximity to a disaster zone—"Here, hold this"—and retreated to the castle in haste, dignity be damned.

Lowen splayed prophetic fingers over his face. "I've said it so many times, Bronnie. You're dangerous. Change him back."

A small, guilty voice: "I don't remember how." With reverent regret she lifted the lid and spoke to the steaming contents. "Sorry."

"He does look so natural," Gwin observed.

Lowen nodded. "All those carrots."

Gwin's suggestion was more than timely. "It's time to go. Lowen, let's get out of here."

"Where?"

"Anywhere. Come on, Bronnie."

They had made rapid escapes before but never in greater need. In mid-run, Bronnie skidded to a halt. "Wait. I can't leave him like this."

She sprinted back to the pot with her promise. "Don't give up hope, Veluvius. I'll practice night and day, day and night until I've brought you back. I'll never give up—"

Even as she vowed, Bronnie was scooped up under each arm by Lowen and Gwin bent on getting lost in a hurry. But Bronnie was a professional and not through. "I'll study and practice and—and if nothing else works, *marry a carrot.*"

And they were offstage, as it were. The founders of the British stage tradition had exited into history.

PARKE GODWIN has written twenty works of fiction, mostly historical and fantasy. In collaboration with Marvin Kaye, he wrote *The Masters of Solitude* and *Wintermind*. A third volume, *Singer Among the Nightingales*, is forthcoming for 2013. Godwin's Arthurian works include *Firelord*, *Beloved Exile* and *The Last Rainbow*. His works on Robin Hood are *Sherwood* and *Robin and the King*. He lives in Auburn, California and is grateful for a background in professional theatre that enabled him to write good dialogue.